VALENTINO'S
LOVE-CHILD

VALENTINO'S LOVE-CHILD

BY

LUCY MONROE

First published in Great Britain 2009
Large Print edition 2009
Harlequin Mills & Boon Limited,
Eton House, 18-24 Paradise Road,
Richmond, Surrey TW9 1SR

© Lucy Monroe 2009

ISBN: 978 0 263 20627 2

Set in Times Roman 16¾ on 19¾ pt.
16-1009-46130

Harlequin Mills & Boon policy is to use papers that are
natural, renewable and recyclable products and made
from wood grown in sustainable forests. The logging and
manufacturing process conform to the legal environmental
regulations of the country of origin.

Printed and bound in Great Britain
by CPI Antony Rowe, Chippenham, Wiltshire

CHAPTER ONE

VALENTINO GRISAFI brushed a silky auburn curl away from where it blocked his view of his sleeping mistress's face.

Mistress. An old-fashioned word for a very modern woman. Faith Williams would not appreciate the label. Were he to be foolish enough to use it within her hearing, she would no doubt let him know it too. His *carina americana* was no wilting flower.

Pretty American. Now, that suited her. But if he should let on he thought of her like a mistress? *Ai-yi-yi.*

Eyes the blue of a peacock feather would snap with temper while she lectured him on how inappropriate the term was. And he supposed she would have a point. He did not pay her bills. He did not buy her clothes. No matter how many hours they spent together here, she did not live in his Marsala apartment. She did not rely on him for anything but his company.

So, not his mistress. But not his girlfriend, either. Long-term commitment and love had no place between them. Theirs was a purely physical relationship, the duration and depth of which was dictated purely by convenience. Mostly his. Not that Faith had nothing to say in the matter.

She could walk away as easily as he and had no more incentive to make time in her schedule for him than vice versa. Luckily for them both, the relationship—such that it was—worked for each of them.

Perhaps they were friends also and he did not regret it, but that had come after. After he had discovered the way her sweet, curvaceous body responded to the slightest touch of his. After kisses that melted his brain and her resistance. After he had learned how much pleasure he could find basking in her generous sensuality, once unleashed.

The sex between them was phenomenal.

Which was no doubt why he could already feel the loss of the coming weeks.

Tracing her perfect oval features he leaned close to her ear. "*Carina,* you must wake."

Her nose wrinkled and the luscious bow of her mouth twisted into a moue of denial, her exotically colored eyes remaining stubbornly closed. Her recently sated body not moving so much as a centimeter from its usual post-coital curled position.

"Come, *bella mia.* Waken."

"If you'd come to my apartment, I could stay in bed sleeping while you had to get dressed and leave," she grumbled into the pillow.

"Most nights, I leave as well, *carina.* You know this." He liked to have breakfast with Giosue. His eight-year-old son was the light of Valentino's life. "Besides, I am not waking you up to go. We need to talk."

Faith's eyelids fluttered, but her mouth did not slip from its downward arch.

"You are adorable like this, you know?"

That had her sitting up and staring at him with grumpy startlement, the tangerine, supersilky,

Egyptian cotton sheet she'd insisted he use on his bed clutched to her chest. "Sane people do not find cranky attractive, Tino."

Biting back a smile, he shrugged. "What can I say? I am different. Or perhaps it is you. I do not recall finding any of my other *amantes* so cute when they were irritable."

He did not like using the word *lover,* but knew better than to refer to her as the equally ill-fitting title of *mistress*. And she had already cut him off at the knees for referring to her once as a bed partner. She said if he wanted to use such a clinical term, he should consider getting an anatomically accurate blow-up doll.

Why these thoughts were plaguing him tonight, he did not know. Defining her place in his life was not something he spent time doing, nor was he overly fond of labels. So why so pre-occupied with them tonight?

"I have no interest in hearing about your past conquests Signor Grisafi." Now she really looked out of sorts, her eyes starting to flash with temper.

"I apologize. But you know I was hardly an

untried boy when we met." He had already loved and lost a wife, not to mention the women who had warmed his cold bed after.

He and Faith had been together for a year, longer than he had been with any other woman since the death of his beloved Renata. But that hardly altered his past.

"Neither of us were virgins, but it's bad form to discuss past relationships while in bed with your current lover."

"You are so worried about following protocols, too," he mocked.

He had never known someone less concerned with appearance and social niceties. His *carina americana* was the quintessential free spirit.

A small smile teased her lips at that. "Maybe not, but this is one social norm I'm one hundred percent behind."

"Duly noted."

"Good." She curled up to him, snuggling against his chest, her hand resting casually on his upper thigh and causing no small reaction in his nether regions. "You said you didn't wake me up to send me on my way?"

"No. We need to talk."

She cocked her head to one side. "What about?"

He couldn't help himself. He leaned down and kissed the tip of her straight nose. "You really are adorable when you first wake up."

"I thought it was when I was grumpy."

"Have you ever woken up *not* irritable?"

"I have a perfectly sunny disposition in the morning. Not that you would know that little fact as we've never spent a full night together, but you'll have to take my word on it. It's only when I have to wake up after being sated so gorgeously with your body that I complain."

It was an old argument. She had never taken his refusal to spend the entire night together with full grace. She understood his desire to be home for breakfast with his son, but not his insistence on leaving their shared bed after at most a short nap after their lovemaking.

Her continued pressing the point frustrated him and that leaked out into his voice when he said, "Be that as it may, there is something I have been meaning to tell you."

She stiffened and pulled away, her blue-green gaze reflecting an instant emotional wariness. "What?"

"It is nothing bad. Well, not too bad. It is simply that my parents are going on a trip. They wish to visit friends in Naples."

"Oh, really? I didn't know."

"Naturally, I did not tell you."

"And?"

"And I cannot leave Giosue at night when he does not have his grandparents there to watch over him." Never mind the staff that lived on site at their vineyard, Vigne di Grisafi, much less the housekeeper that had her own room in the house. It was not the same.

"I understand." He could tell from her expression that she really did. "How long will your parents be gone?"

"Two weeks only."

"I won't see you at all?"

"It is unlikely."

She looked like she wanted to say something, but in the end she simply nodded.

"I will miss you," he found himself admitting. Then he scowled. He hadn't wanted to say that.

"This." He brushed his hand down her body. "I will miss *this*."

"I heard you the first time, tough guy. You can't take it back now. You may as well admit you like my company as much as me in your bed."

He bore her back to the bed, his mouth hovering above hers. "Maybe almost as much. And speaking of sex. I will have to do without you for two weeks, I think we should take advantage of our time together."

"Have I ever said no to you?" she asked with a husky laugh.

"No and tonight is no time to start."

Faith woke surrounded by warmth and the scent of the man she loved.

Her eyes flew open and a grin split her face. It hadn't been a dream. After making love into the wee hours of the morning, Tino had asked her to spend the night. For the first time ever.

Okay, maybe not asked…more like informed her that she was staying, but it was the same result. She was in his arms, in his bed—the morning after they'd made love.

And it was glorious.

Every bit as delicious a feeling as she had thought it would be.

"Are you awake?" his deep voice rumbled above her.

She lifted her head from its resting place on his hair-covered chest and turned the full wattage of her smile on him. "What does it look like?"

"It looks like you were telling me the truth when you said you had a sunny disposition in the morning. Maybe I will have to start calling you *solare*."

Sunlight? Her heart squeezed. "Tay used to call me Sunshine."

"A past boyfriend?" Tino asked on a growl, the morning whiskers on his face giving him a sexily fierce aspect. "You are right, discussing past *amores* while in bed with your current one is definitely bad taste."

She laughed, not in the least offended. "He was my husband, not a past boyfriend," she said as she scooted out of the bed, intent on making coffee.

"You were married?"

"Yes." Weird that after almost a full year together, she was telling him about having been married before for the first time. But then, that was the nature of their relationship. She and Tino focused on the present when they were together.

She'd learned more about him—and a tragic past similar to her own—from his mother than she'd ever learned from him. Strangely enough, where Tino showed no interest in Faith's art, his mother was a fan. They'd met at one of Faith's showings in Palermo. In spite of the generation difference in their ages, the two women had hit it off immediately and both had been thrilled to discover they lived so close to one another. Vigne di Grisafi was a mere twenty-minute drive from Faith's small apartment in Pizzolato.

Not that she'd ever been there as Tino's guest. She'd been seeing Tino for two months before she realized the Valentino Agata mentioned so frequently was Tino, the man Faith spent her nights making love with. At first, she'd found it disconcerting, but she'd soon adjusted. She hadn't told Agata about the fact she was dating Tino though.

He'd been careful to keep their relationship discreet and she felt it was his prerogative to determine when his family would be told about her.

In another almost unreal twist of fate, Faith was his son Giosue's teacher, too. She taught an art class for primary school children in Marsala once a week. She may have lost her one chance at motherhood, but she still adored kids, and this was her way of spending time with them. Giosue was an absolute doll and she more than understood Tino's desire to be there for him. She applauded it.

"Divorced?" Tino asked, his brown eyes intent on her and apparently not done with the topic of Tay.

"Widowed." She didn't elaborate, knowing Tino wouldn't want the details. He never wanted the details. Not about her personal history.

He said he liked to concentrate on the here and now. Since that was her own personal motto, she didn't balk at the fact he showed no interest in her life before Sicily. She had to admit, though, that he didn't show much interest in her life here, either.

He knew she was an artist, but she wasn't sure

he knew she was a successful one or that she was a clay sculptor. He knew she lived in Pizzolato, a small town a few minutes south of Marsala, but she doubted he knew exactly where her apartment was. In the entire year they'd been together, they had made love in one place only—his apartment.

Not his home, because he didn't live there. He said he kept it for business purposes, but she thought he meant the business of getting sex without falling under the watchful eye of his mother. Tino had been very careful to keep their lives completely separate.

At first, she hadn't minded. She'd been no more interested in a deep emotional connection than he had been. He'd promised her sex and that was all he'd given her.

Only, at some point along the way, she'd realized, she couldn't help giving him love.

Even so, she'd been content to keep their relationship on a shallow level. Or at least convinced herself to be. She'd lost everyone she'd ever loved and had no doubt that one day she would lose him, too. That didn't mean she hadn't loved spending the whole night together—she had. But as for the rest of it, the less entwined in her life he was, the better for her it would be when that time came.

At least, that was how she had thought. She wasn't so sure anymore.

"So, that is all you have to say on the matter?"

She pushed the start button on the coffee-maker and turned to face Tino. "What?"

He'd pulled on a pair of boxers, leaving most of his tall, chiseled body on mouthwatering display. "Your husband died."

Were they still on that? "Yes."

"How?"

"A car accident."

"When?"

"Six years ago."

He ran his fingers through his morning tousled dark hair. "You never told me."

"Did you want me to?"

"I would think that sometime in a year you would have thought to mention that you were a widow." He came into the kitchen and leaned against the counter near her.

"Why?"

"It is an important piece of information about you."

"About my past."

He frowned at her.

"You prefer to focus on today, not yesterday. You've said so many times, Tino. What's going on?"

"Maybe I'm just curious about the woman I've been bedding for a year."

"Almost a year."

"Do not banter semantics with me."

"I'm glad you're curious."

"I…" For the first time in memory, her lover, the über-cool Valentino Grisafi, looked lost for words.

"Don't worry about it, Tino. It's not a bad thing."

"No, no, of course not. We are friends as well as lovers, *si?*"

"Yes." And she was more relieved than she could say that he saw it that way, too.

"Good. Good." He was silent a second. "Do I get breakfast to go with my coffee?"

"I think that can be arranged."

He got a borderline horrified look on his face. "You do know how to cook, don't you?"

She laughed, truly tickled. "We aren't all filthy rich vintners, Tino. Some of us can't afford a housekeeper or to eat out every meal—thus, knowing how to cook is essential. But I don't mind telling you, I'm pretty good at it as well."

"I'll reserve judgment."

She laughed and launched herself at him to tickle the big man into submission, or at least a lot of laughter before he subdued her wandering fingers.

Faith finished the third form of a pregnant woman she had done in as many days. She hadn't done women *enceinte* since the loss of her baby in the accident that had killed Taylish and any chance Faith would ever have at a family.

Or so she had believed.

Her clay-spattered hand pressed over her still-flat stomach, a sense of awe and wonder infusing her. It had taken her four years and fertility counseling for her to become viably pregnant the first time.

Her first actual pregnancy had occurred a mere two months after she married Taylish at the age of eighteen. They'd been ecstatic when the home pregnancy test showed positive, only to be cast into a pit of despair short weeks later when the ectopic pregnancy had come close to killing her. And of course, there had been no hope of saving the baby with a tubal pregnancy.

Her near death had not stopped her and Tay from trying again. They both wanted children with a deep desperation only those who had no family could appreciate. After a year of trying with no results they'd sought medical help. Tests had revealed that she'd been left with only one working ovary in the aftermath of her ectopic pregnancy.

The fertility specialist she and Tay had sought out had informed them that the single working ovary significantly decreased their chances at getting pregnant. However, she gave them a regime to follow that would hopefully result in conception. It had been grueling and resulted in an already passionless sex life turning flat-out clinical.

But it had worked. When the test strip had turned blue, she'd felt as if it was the greatest blessing of her life. This time she'd felt as if it was a full-on miracle.

Tino was careful to use condoms every time. The number of chances they'd taken by waiting to put the condom on until after some play, and the single time one had broken (Tino had changed where he bought his condoms after that), could be counted on one hand. With fingers left over. However, one of those times of delayed sheathing had occurred a couple of months ago.

With only one working ovary, her menstrual cycles were on an erratic two-month schedule. She hadn't paid any attention when her sporadic period was later than even normal. It wasn't the first time. Pregnancy had never even crossed her mind. Not when her breasts had grown excessively tender. She'd put it up to PMS. Not when the smell of bacon made her nauseous. She wasn't a huge meat eater, anyway.

Not when she got tired in the afternoons. After all, most Sicilian businesses were closed for a couple of hours midday so people could rest.

Maybe she was just taking on the habits of her adopted home. She hadn't even clued in she might be pregnant when she burst out crying over a broken glass one morning when she'd been preparing a heavier breakfast than usual. She'd been craving eggs.

The shoe hadn't even dropped when she made her fourth trip to the bathroom before lunchtime one day. She'd made an appointment to see her doctor to test for a suspected bladder infection, only to be stunned with the news she was carrying Tino's child.

She pressed against her hard tummy with a reverent hand. All the symptoms of pregnancy now carried special significance for her. She, a woman who'd had every chance at family she'd ever had ripped from her by death, was expecting. It was almost impossible to believe she'd been so blind to the possibility. With her fertility problems, Faith had assumed there wasn't even a remote chance she could or would ever get pregnant again.

Yet, according to the test her doctor had run, she was. *She was.*

Oh, man.

She hugged herself while looking down at the faceless pregnant figure she'd been working on. The incredible awe and joy she felt at the prospect of having a baby—Tino's baby—could be seen in every line of the figure whose arms were raised above her head in an unmistakable gesture of celebration. Faith turned to look at the first woman she'd done after finding out she was pregnant.

That figure showed the fear that laced her joy. This woman had a face, and her expression was one of trepidation. Her hand rested protectively on her slightly protruding stomach. Faith had done the woman as a native African. Clinging to one side of her traditional dress was another small child, not so thin it was starving, but clearly at risk. The two figures were standing on a base that had been created to look like dry grass.

It was a moving statue, bringing tears to her own eyes. Which wasn't exactly something new. The one place Faith allowed herself to express her inner pain, the feelings of aloneness that she accepted but had never quite learned to live with, was her art. While some pieces were filled with joy and peace, others evoked the kind of emotion few people liked to talk about.

Despite that—or maybe because of it—her art sold well, commanding a high price for each piece. Or at least each one she allowed to leave her workshop. The pregnant woman she'd done yesterday wasn't going anywhere but back into a lump of clay. It was too jumbled a piece. No single emotional connotation strong enough to override the others.

Some work was like that. She accepted it as the cost of her process. She'd spent the entire day on that statue, but not late into the night like she had on the first one. Part of it was probably the fact that Tino had called her.

He rarely called her, except to set up assignations. Even when he traveled out of country and was gone for a week or more, she did not hear from him. But he had called yesterday. For no other reason she could discern other than to talk. Weird.

Really, really.

But good. Any loosening of his strictly sex relationship rule was a blessing. Especially now.

But still. Odd.

She wasn't sure when she was going to tell him about the baby. She had no doubts she would do so, but wanted to time it right. There was always a chance of miscarriage in the first trimester, and with her track record she wasn't going to dismiss that very real possibility. She'd lost every chance she'd had for a family up to now, it was hard to believe that this time would work out any differently.

She could still hope, though.

That didn't mean she was going to share news of the baby before she was sure her pregnancy was viable. She had an appointment with the hospital later in the week. Further tests would determine whether the pregnancy was uteral rather than ectopic. Though her original fertility specialist had told her the chances of having another tubal pregnancy were so slim as to be almost nonexistent, Faith wasn't taking any chances.

And she wasn't telling Tino anything until she was sure.

CHAPTER TWO

THE day before her appointment at the hospital was Faith's day to teach art to the primary schoolers. She'd fallen into the job by accident. Sort of. Faith had told Agata Grisafi how much she loved children and spending time with them, but of course her career did not lend itself to doing so. The older woman had spoken to the principal of her grandson's school and discovered he would be thrilled to have a successful artist come in and teach classes one day a week to his students.

That's how it had begun and how Faith had ended up knowing her lover's mother and son longer than she'd known him. Some people might say Providence had lent a hand, and Faith thought maybe, just maybe they might be right.

Giosue, Tino's darling eight-year-old son, was in the second group she taught for the day.

He was his normal sweet self, shyly asking her opinion of the drawing he had done of Marsala's city hall. They were doing a project combining their writing skills and art to give a picture of their city as eight- and nine-year-olds saw it.

"That's beautiful, Gio."

"Thank you, *signora.*"

She moved on to the next child, helping the little girl pick a color for the fish she wanted to draw in the sea so close to Marsala.

It was at the end of class, after all the other children had left, that Giosue came to her desk. "Signora Guglielmo?"

The children called her by the Italian equivalent of William rather than Williams because it was easier for them and she didn't mind a bit.

"Yes, sweetheart?"

He grinned at the endearment, his cheeks pinkening a little, but so obviously pleased that she made a note to use it again. Sparingly.

No matter how special the place in her heart Tino's son had, she would not draw attention to it. To do so would embarrass Giosue, most likely infuriate Tino and compromise Faith's position with the school.

"I would like to invite you to join my family for dinner tonight," he said formally. It was clear he'd practiced the phrase, as well.

"Does your father know you are inviting me to dinner?" she asked, seriously concerned by this turn of events.

"Yes, *signora*. He would be very pleased if you came."

Shock slammed through her. "Did he say that?"

"Oh, yes." Giosue gave her another of his shy smiles. "He is very pleased I like you so well."

Hope bubbled through her like an effervescent spring. Perhaps the black cloud over her life was finally dissipating. Was it possible she had a chance at a real family once again—one that would not be taken away from her? The hope scared her so much it hurt. "I would be honored to join you for dinner."

"Thank you, *signora*." Giosue handed her a folded sheet of paper. "My father made you directions for coming, in case you need them."

She took the paper. "Thank you, I appreciate that."

She'd been there a few times for lunch with Agata, though the older woman preferred to meet in Pizzolato because she loved visiting Faith's studio. She said she basked in the privilege of seeing the artist's work before it was finished.

"It was my idea to make the map. I helped Papa with it."

That was her cue to open it and marvel over the drawing, which had obviously been done by a child's hand. The detailed written instructions were in Tino's distinctive slashing scrawl, however.

"You did a wonderful job, Gio. I particularly like the grapevines with grapes on them you drew to show me what to expect to see."

"They are ripening on the vines now. Nonno said they will be ready to harvest when he gets back from Naples maybe."

"If your grandfather says it, than I am sure he is right."

"He is a master winemaker," Giosue said proudly.

"Yes. Do you help with the harvest?"

"Some. Nonno takes me into the fields with him. Papa does not work the fields, but that is okay. Nonno says so."

"Your father's gift is for the business side of things, I think."

"Nonno says Papa is very good at making money," Giosue replied artlessly.

Faith laughed. "I'm sure he is."

"He can support a family. Nonna says so."

"I'm sure he can." Was Giosue matchmaking? Faith held in the smile that wanted to break over her features. She did not want to hurt Giosue by making him think she was laughing at him.

"She thinks he should marry again. She is his mama, he has to listen to her, I think."

It was really hard to bite back the laugh at that, but she did not think Tino would share his son's view on this particular subject. "What do you think, Gio?"

"I think I would like a mother who is not so far away in Heaven."

She couldn't help it. She reached out and touched him. Just a small pat on the shoulder, but she wanted to hug him to her. "I understand, Gio. I really do."

He cocked his head to one side. "You never talk about family."

"I don't have any." Her hand slid down to her stomach. She hadn't. Before. But now, maybe she did.

"You have no mama, either?"

"No. I prayed for one, but it was not God's will." She shrugged.

"Do you think I will have another mother?"

"I hope so, Gio."

"Me, too, but only if I could love her."

Smart boy. "I'm sure your father wouldn't marry a woman you couldn't love as a mama, too."

"She would have to love me also." Giosue looked at her through his lashes, worrying his lower lip with his teeth.

Sweet little boy. "You are very lovable, that would not be a problem, I'm sure."

The next group of children came rushing into the room along with Giosue's teacher, who was apparently looking for her missing lamb.

"I will see you tonight?" he asked as crossed the room to join his teacher at the door.

"Yes."

He was grinning as he exited the room.

So, Tino's son *was* matchmaking. With her. And seemingly, he had Tino's tacit approval. Unbelievable. The prospect terrified her as much as it thrilled her. Had she suffered enough? Was she done being alone?

Somehow, she couldn't quite picture it.

If nothing else, Tino was allowing her into another aspect of his life. The most important one to him. That was so huge, she could barely wrap her mind around it.

The fact that he was doing so without knowing about the baby boggled her mind even more.

He might not love her, but she had a different place in his life than any woman had since the death of his wife six years ago.

Faith concentrated on the strains of classical music filling her Mini. At least, she tried to. She was extremely nervous about this dinner. She shouldn't be. Over the past year, they'd discovered that she and Tino were compatible in and out of bed. She and Giosue got along great in the classroom as well. It should all be good.

Only, telling herself that didn't make the butterflies playing techno music in her stomach go away. This was the two of them together. Tino *and* Giosue. The three of them really.

How they interacted would dictate a big chunk of her future; she was sure of it. Tino had to be testing the waters and, as absolutely inconceivable as she found that, it sort of fit in with his odd behavior lately.

He'd called her again today. She'd missed the call and when she'd tried to return it he'd been in a meeting. His message had simply said he'd been thinking of her.

Seriously strange.

If he'd said he'd been thinking of sex with her, she wouldn't have been surprised at all. The man had the libido of an eighteen-year-old. Sex was a really important part of his life. Important enough that he pursued it even though he had said he never wanted to remarry or get serious with a woman.

But he hadn't said he was missing the sex. He'd said he was missing *her*. Well, they would be together again soon enough. And then they would see what they would see.

Her phone rang, playing his distinctive ring tone. She never answered when she was driving, so she forced herself to ignore it. Besides, she was almost to Grisafi Vineyard. He could say whatever he wanted when she got there. Most likely, he was calling to see where she was.

But she wasn't late.

Well, not much, anyway. Maybe ten minutes. He had to be used to her sketchy time-keeping skills by now. It was one of the reasons that she loved living in Sicily. Tino was very un-Sicilian in his perfect punctuality and rigid schedule keeping. She'd teased him about it more than once.

He'd told her he had no choice, doing business on an international scale. She suspected it was in his nature and that was that.

She couldn't see Tino changing for the convenience of others, not even when it came to making money.

She turned down the long drive that led to Casa di Fede. Faith House. She'd thought it was neat the house shared her name when she'd first come to visit Agata. Later, when she realized Tino lived here, she'd seen it as an indication they were meant to be together. Even if it was temporary.

Thinking about the coincidence sent another bubble of hope fizzing through her. Maybe it meant something more than what she'd thought. He and his family were wrapped around her life, and she was threaded through his, in ways neither had anticipated or even wanted at first.

She pulled up in front of the sprawling farm house. It had been in the family for six generations and been built onto almost that number of times until it had two master suites, one in its own wing with two additional bedrooms. There were four more bedrooms in the rest of the house, a formal salon, a family entertainment room that opened onto the lanai beside the oversize two-tiered pool and spa area, a huge kitchen, a library and two offices.

One was Tino's, and the smaller, less-organized one was his father's. Agata used the library as her office when she was working on her charity work. She had her own sitting room off the master suite, as well.

Faith had learned all of this on her previous visits with the older woman. What she hadn't known was how overwhelming she would find the familiar home now that she was here to share dinner with Tino and his son. She sat in her car, staring at the proof of generations of Grisafis living in the same area. Proof of Tino's roots and his wealth. Proof that he already had what she had most craved her whole life.

A family.

The prospect that he might be willing to share all that with her was almost more than she could take. Terrifying didn't begin to describe it. Because even if Valentino Grisafi wanted her in his life, she of all people knew there was no guarantee she could keep him. No more than she'd kept the father she never knew, or her mother, or the first family that said they would adopt her, or Taylish…or her unborn son, Kaden.

Dwelling on the pain of the past had never helped her before; she knew it wasn't about to start now. She needed to let the past go and hope for the future, or her own fears were going to destroy her chance at happiness.

With that resolved, she opened her car door. Her phone trilled Tino's ringtone again as she stepped out of the car.

She flipped it open. "Wow, I know you're impatient, but this is borderline obsessive, Tino. I'm here already."

"I merely wished to—"

She rang the bell and he stopped talking.

"It is the doorbell. I must let you go."

Shaking her head at that, she shrugged and disconnected the call.

He opened the door and then stood there staring at her as if she was an apparition—of not particularly friendly aspect. In truth, he looked absolutely horrified.

"Faith!"

"The last time I looked, yes."

"What are you doing here?" He shook his head. "It does not matter. You need to leave. Now."

"What? Why?"

"This is my fault." He rubbed his hand over his face. "I can see where my phone calls may have given you the wrong impression."

"That you might be impatient to see me?"

"Yes, I am. I was. But not here. Not now."

"Tino, you aren't making any sense."

"This is not a good time, Faith. I need you to leave now."

"Won't Gio be disappointed?"

"Gio…why would you ask about my son? Look, it doesn't matter, we have a dinner guest coming."

She rolled her eyes. "Yes, I know. I'm here."

"This is no time for jokes, *carina*."

"Tino, you're starting to worry me." Really. Definitely. Positive that Giosue would not lie and say his father had approved inviting her for dinner, she was flummoxed. Besides, hadn't Tino helped his son make the map? What was going on? "Tino—"

"Signora!" An excited little boy voice broke into the bizarre conversation. "You are here!"

Giosue rushed past his father to throw his arms around Faith in a hug. She returned the embrace with a smile, loving the naturally affectionate nature of most of the Sicilians she had met.

Tino stood there looking at them in abject horror.

Giosue stepped back, self-consciously straightening his button-up shirt. He'd dressed up for the dinner in an outfit close to the uniform he wore to school of obviously higher quality and minus the tie. He looked like a miniature version of his father, who was wearing custom-tailored brown slacks with a champagne colored dress shirt—untucked, the top button undone.

The clothes were absolutely yummy on the father and adorable on the son.

Faith was glad she'd taken the time to change from the clothing she wore to teach in. Her dress was made from yellow silk batiked by a fellow artist with strands of peacock blue, sunset orange and even a metallic dye with a gold cast. Faith had fallen in love with the silk when she'd seen it at an artists' fair and had to buy it. She'd had it made into a dress of simple design with spaghetti straps that highlighted her curves and made her feel deliciously feminine. A new addition to her wardrobe, Tino had not yet seen it.

Regardless of his other reactions to her arrival, that certain gleam she knew so well in her lover's eyes said he approved her choice.

Unaware of the strange overtones to the adults' conversation, Gio took her hand and held it. "Papa, this is Signora Guglielmo." Then the boy smiled up at her with pure innocence. "*Signora,* this is my papa, Signor Valentino Grisafi."

"Your papa and I have met," Faith said, when Tino remained silent and frozen like a statue. An appalled statue.

"You have?" Gio looked confused, maybe even a little hurt. "Papa told me he did not know you. Nonna told him he would like you though."

"I did not realize that Signora Guglielmo was the woman *I* know as Faith Williams." He looked at her accusingly, as if it was her fault.

"You are friends?" Giosue asked.

Faith waited to hear what her lover would say to that.

Tino looked from her to his son, his expression impossible to read. "*Si.* We are friends."

Giosue's face broke out into a grin and he giggled. "You didn't know? Truly?"

"Truly."

"That is a good joke, isn't it, Papa?"

"A good joke indeed," Tino agreed, sounding anything but amused.

Faith wasn't feeling too lighthearted, either. Tino hadn't approved inviting *her* for dinner. He hadn't written those directions out with *her* in mind to use them. He'd had no intention of inviting her into an aspect of his life he had heretofore kept separate from her. In fact, he was clearly dismayed and not at all happy by this evening's turn of events.

He'd approved inviting *his son's teacher.* Another woman. A woman who Tino would have been told by his son and mother was single, near him in age and attractive (or so Agata said every time she lamented Faith's unwed state). If the fact that Giosue had been matchmaking was obvious to Faith, it had to have been just as apparent to his father. Add to that the little detail that Agata had patently put her two cents in, and Faith was painting a picture in her mind that held no gratification for her.

Tino had approved inviting to dinner a woman his son and mother were obviously hoping he would find more than a little interesting.

All of the little pipe dreams Faith had been building since spending the night for the first time at Tino's flat, crashed and burned.

But she wasn't a wimp. Far from it. She'd taken a lot more that life had to dish out without giving up. She was here now. And she had important motivation to make this evening work in spite of her lover's negative reaction to her appearance.

Perhaps if Tino saw how good they could be together around his family, he'd rethink the parameters on their relationship. Then telling him about the baby wouldn't be so hard.

And maybe the Peruvian rain forest would freeze over in a freak weather anomaly tonight, too.

Okay, that kind of negative thinking wasn't going to do her any good. She had to think positive. No matter what, she wasn't about to beg off dinner. That would hurt Giosue, and Faith didn't let children down. Ever.

She'd experienced that particular phenomenon too many times herself to inflict it on the young people in her life.

She gave both males her best winning smile and asked, "May I come in now, or were you planning to have dinner on the front porch?"

Giosue laughed and dragged her over the threshold, forcing his father to move out of the way or get knocked into. "We're eating outside, but in back, silly *signora.*"

"And did you cook, Gio?"

"I helped. Ask Papa."

She looked back over her shoulder at the silent man following their progress through the house.

"Indeed he did. He is a favorite with our housekeeper."

"It's easy to understand why. Gio's a little charmer."

"Signora!" Gio exclaimed in the long-suffering tone only an eight-year-old boy could affect so perfectly.

"Do not tell me it embarrasses you to discover

your favorite teacher also holds you in high regard," his father teased him.

The boy shrugged, blushing, but said nothing. Faith's heart melted a little more toward him. He would make such a wonderful stepson and big brother. But she was getting ahead of herself. By light-years.

"So, what are we having for dinner?" she asked.

Especially after realizing Tino had not intended to invite her to dinner. That he had, in fact, been wholly ignorant of her relationship with his son and mother.

"Wait until you see. I got to stuff the manicotti. The filling is yummy."

Giosue was right, the manicotti was delicious. As was everything else, and the company wasn't bad, either. Tino started off a little stiff, but being around his son relaxed him. As hard as he so plainly tried to keep things between himself and Faith distant, his usual behavior got the better of him. He touched her when he talked to her, nothing overtly sexual. Just the normal affectionate-Sicilian-nature style, but it felt good—right.

Gio asked tons of questions about her art, questions there wasn't time for during class. Several times she caught Tino looking surprised by her answers. But then, he knew almost nothing about that part of her life. For the first time that really bothered her. Her art made up the biggest part of her life and he was sadly ignorant of it.

That realization, more than anything else, put the nature of their relationship into perspective. While his behavior lately might indicate it was changing, theirs was still primarily a sexually based connection.

"You are asking so many questions, *amorino,* I am beginning to think you wish to grow up to be an artist."

"Oh, no, Papa, I want to be a winemaker like Nonno."

"Not a businessman and vintner like your papa?" Faith asked.

"He will have to have another son to do that. I want to get my hands dirty," Giosue said with absolute certainty.

Rather than take offense, Tino laughed aloud.

"He sounds just like my father." He shook his head, the amusement still glittering in his eyes. "However, there will be no brothers, or sisters either. Perhaps Calogero will finally marry and have children, but if not—when I get too old to do my job, we will have to hire a business manager."

"You will never be too old, Papa."

Tino just smiled and ruffled his son's hair. "You know there is nothing to stop you from making art a hobby while you follow in your grandfather's footsteps. Isn't that right, Faith?"

She was still reeling from the dead-on surety in Tino's tone when he said there would be no sisters or brothers for Giosue, but she managed to nod and smile at the expectant little boy.

CHAPTER THREE

TINO rejoined Faith on the terrace after tucking his son into bed.

Gio had wheedled, pleaded and distracted every time Faith had started making noises about going home. When it was finally time for *him* to go to bed, he had even gone so far as to ask to have her come in and say good-night to him before going to sleep.

She'd done so without the slightest hesitation, kissing Gio's head before wishing him a good sleep and pleasant dreams and then leaving the room. Tino found it disconcerting that she was so relaxed, not to mention good, with his son. Their friendship was of longstanding duration, and he wasn't sure how he felt about that. Except uncomfortable.

He didn't like feeling unsettled. It made him irritable.

And it wasn't at all cute, like his lover when she was woken to go home after an evening of lovemaking.

Faith stood on the edge of the stone terrace, looking out over the vineyard. The green, leafy vines looked black in the moonlight, but she glowed. The cool illumination of the night sky reflected off her porcelain features, lending her a disturbing, ethereal beauty. She looked like an angelic specter that could be snatched to the other realms in the blink of an eye.

It was not a thought he wanted to entertain. Not after that very thing had happened to Maura through her death. The one challenge to their life together that he could not fight.

He was frowning when he laid his hand on Faith's shoulder. "He is on his way to dreamland."

"He's so incredibly sweet. You are a very blessed man, Valentino Grisafi." She turned to face him.

"I know it." He sighed. "But there are times he puts me in an inconvenient situation."

"Like when he invites your current lover to dinner?"

"Yes."

She winced. "You could have said no."

"So could you."

"I thought you wanted me here."

"*I* thought he had invited his teacher from school."

"I am his teacher," she chided. "His art teacher, anyway."

"Why did you never mention this to me?" It seemed almost contrived to him.

"How could you *not* know? I mean, I'm aware you are supremely uninterested in my life outside our time together, but I've mentioned teaching art to primary schoolers in Marsala."

"I thought you did it to support your art *hobby*. My mother told me Gio's teacher was a highly successful artist who donated her time." Realizing how wrong he'd been made him feel like fool.

Another unpleasant and infrequent experience. Grisafi men did not make a habit of ignorance or stupid behavior. His pride stung at the knowledge he was guilty of both. Knowing more about Faith would have saved him the current situation.

"And in your eyes I could not be that woman?" Faith asked in that tone all men knew was very dangerous.

The one that said a husband would be sleeping on the sofa for the foreseeable future. Faith was not his wife, but he didn't want to be cut off from her body, nevertheless. Nor did he wish to offend her in any case.

"In my eyes, that woman, Signora Guglielmo, was Sicilian—and you are not."

"No, I'm not. Is that a problem for you, Tino?"

Where had that question come from? He was no ethnic supremacist. "Patently not. We have been lovers for a year now, Faith."

"Almost a year."

"Near enough."

"I suppose, but I'm trying to understand why my being a Sicilian art teacher would make me an appropriate dinner companion for you and your son, but being your expatriot American lover does not."

"It will not work."

"What?"

"Attempting to use Giosue to insinuate yourself into my life more deeply than I wish you to go."

Hurt sparked in her peacock eyes, and then anger. "Don't be paranoid, not to mention criminally conceited. One, I would never use a child—in any way. Two, I knew your son before I met you. What would you have had me do? Start ignoring him in class once you and I had become lovers?"

"Of course not." He sighed. What a tangle. "But you could have discouraged outright friendship."

"We were already friends. It would never occur to me to hurt a child with rejection that way. I won't do it now, either, Tino, not even for you."

"That is not what I meant."

"Then what *did* you mean?"

He swore. He wasn't sure, and that was as disturbing as any other revelation from this night. He fell back on what he considered the topic at hand. "Let's not make this more complicated than we need to. You know I do not allow the women I sleep with into my personal life. It would be too messy."

Cocking her head to one side, she gave him a look filled with disbelief. "You don't consider what we do together as personal?"

"You are nit-picking semantics here, Faith. You know what I am meaning here. Why are you being willfully obtuse? You knew the limitations of our relationship from the very beginning." She was not normally so argumentative, and why she had to start being so now was a mystery to him.

Certainly she had strong opinions, but they were not, as a rule, in opposition to his.

"Maybe I'm no longer happy with them." She watched him as if gauging his reaction to that bombshell.

Alarm bells for a five-alarm fire went off in his head. Her words filled him with pure panic—not an emotion he was used to feeling and not one he had predisposed reactions for. "Faith, you must understand something. I have no plans to remarry. Ever."

"I know, but—"

Those three little words sent a shard of apprehension right through him. She could not keep thinking in this manner. "If I did remarry, it would be to a traditional Sicilian woman—like Giosue's mother."

Some Sicilian men married American women, but it was rare. Even rarer still, almost to the point of nonexistent, were Sicilian men who continued to live on the island after marrying them.

Regardless, *were* he to remarry, he felt compelled to provide a female influence as like Giosue's real mother as possible. He owed it to Maura.

Being honest with himself would require he acknowledge that his reasons were not limited to cultural gaps and the obligation he felt to his dead wife, but had as much to do with a promise to keep. Only one woman put his promise to Maura at risk, his promise not to replace his wife, who had died too young in his heart.

And that woman was a smart, sexy American.

Faith crossed her arms, as if protecting herself from a blow. "Is that why you didn't nip your son's obvious attempt at matchmaking in the bud? Because you believed the woman he was trying to fix you up with was Sicilian?"

"Yes." He could not lie, though the temptation was there.

This time Faith didn't just wince, she flinched as if struck. "I see."

"I don't think you do." Needing her understanding—her acceptance—he cupped her face with both hands. "My son is the most important person in my life, I would do anything for him."

"Even remarry."

"If I believed that was what he truly needed for happiness, yes." But not to a woman who would expect access to more than his body and bank account. Not to a woman who already threatened his memories of Maura and his promise to her.

Not Faith.

"Do you?"

Again wishing he could lie, he dropped his hands. "I did not, but after tonight, I am not so sure. He loves his grandmother, but he glowed under your affection in a way that he does not with his nonna."

"He's very special to me."

"If he is so special, why did you not tell me he was your student?"

"You already asked that and the simple truth is that I thought you knew. I assumed he and, well, your mother, talked about me. We are friends. I suppose that's going to send you into another tizzy of paranoia, but please remember, she and I were friends before I even met Gio."

"You and…and…my *mother?*"

"Yes."

Tonight had been one unreal revelation after another. "You did not tell me this."

"I thought you knew," she repeated, sounding exasperated. She turned away from him. "Perhaps Agata and I are not as close as I assumed."

The sad tone in Faith's voice did something strange to Tino's heart. He did not like it. At all. He was used to her being happy most of the time—sometimes cranky but never sad. It did not fit her.

"She did talk about you, but I did not realize it was *you* she was talking about." His mother had mentioned Gio's teacher on occasion. Not often, though, and he too wondered if the two women shared as close a friendship as Faith believed.

His mother was a true patron of the arts. She had many acquaintances in the artistic community. He could easily see her warm nature and natural graciousness being mistaken for friendship. But the only artist she mentioned often was TK.

For a while, Tino had been worried his mother had developed a *tendre* for the male artist. However, when he had mentioned his concern to his father, Rosso Grisafi had laughed until tears came to his eyes. Tino had drawn the conclusion that clearly there was nothing to worry about.

"That's hardly my fault, Tino."

"I did not say it was."

"You implied it by asking why I didn't tell you."

What was it with her tonight and this taking apart everything that he said? "You are apparently very close to both my mother and my son and yet you never once mentioned seeing or talking to them."

"You always discourage me from discussing your family, Tino."

It was true, but for some reason, the reminder bothered him. Probably because everything was leaving him feeling disconcerted tonight. "I did not think they had a place in our combined life."

"We don't have a combined life, do we, Tino?" She was looking at him again and he almost wished she wasn't.

There was such defeat and sadness in her eyes.

"I do not understand what has changed between us?"

"Nothing. Nothing at all has changed between us."

"Then why are you sad?"

"Perhaps because I thought it had."

Why had she believed this?

"You were under the impression I wanted you to come for dinner tonight," he said, understanding beginning to dawn. Clearly she had liked the idea. Learning differently had hurt her. Even though he had not meant for this to happen, he had to take some responsibility for the outcome.

She nodded, silent, her lovely red hair swaying against her shoulders. He had the wholly inappropriate—considering the gravity of their discussion—urge to run his fingers through the familiar silky strands. Worse, he knew he did not want to stop there.

Focus, he must focus.

"It is not good for Giosue to be exposed to my lovers."

"I understand you think that."

"It is the truth."

She said nothing.

He could not leave it there. The compulsion to explain—to make her understand—was too great. "When our relationship ends, he will be disappointed. Already he has expectations that cannot be fulfilled."

"I'm his friend."

"He wants you to be his mother."

"And you don't."

"No." It was a knee-jerk response, the result of ingrained beliefs since his wife's death.

Shocking to realize he wasn't sure he meant it. With that came grief—a sense of loss that made no sense and was something he was not even remotely willing to dwell on.

"Because I'm not Sicilian."

"Because our relationship is not a love affair."
But was that true?

How could it be anything else when he *could
not* love her? He had promised Maura that he
would love her always. Her sudden death had
not negated that pledge.

"I thought we were friends, too."

"We are friends." Friendship he could do—
was necessary even.

"But not sweethearts."

His heart twinged, making his tone come out
more cynical than he meant it to. "What an old-
fashioned term."

She shrugged. "It's one Tay used to use." She
said the dead man's name with a wistfulness
that he did not like.

"I gather he was an unusual man."

"Yes. He was. One of the best, maybe even the
best man I ever knew."

"But he is *gone*."

"Yes, just as Gio's mother is gone."

"Maura will never be gone from my heart."

"No, she won't, but are you so sure your heart
has no room for anyone else?"

"That is not a discussion you and I should be having." It was one he frankly could not handle.

A Sicilian man should be able to handle anything. Even the death of his wife and raising his child without a mother. But most definitely any conversation with his current mistress. The fact that he could not shamed him.

"Because we agreed that sex and friendship was enough?" she asked in a voice husky with emotion.

"Yes."

"And if it isn't any longer...*for either of us?*"

That could not be true. He would not allow it to be. "Do not presume to speak for me."

"Fine. What if I am only speaking for myself?"

"Then we would need to talk about whether what we have is still working." It was not a discussion he wanted to have. He was far from ready to let her go.

She nodded and turned from him. "I think it's time I was going." She was hurting, for all that she tried to hide it.

"No." He hated the melancholy in her voice.

He hated the sense that somehow it was his fault. He hated thinking of going to bed alone after spending the whole evening in her company. Even worse, he hated feeling as if he might lose her and *really* hated how much that bothered him.

Perhaps he could erase her sorrow while easing his own fears. He was a big proponent of the win-win business proposition. It was even better when applied to personal relationships.

Before she could take more than a couple of steps, he reached out and caught her shoulder.

"Tino, don't."

"You do not mean that, *carina*." He drew her back toward his body. He could not imagine doing the opposite—pushing her away.

Yet he knew he could not hold on to her forever. One day she would tire of life in Sicily—so different from her home—and would return to America. Isn't that what all American women did eventually?

Faith was currently the only single American woman he knew who was making a go of actually living permanently in Sicily. For all its charm, Marsala was a far cry from New York or London.

That only meant they should not waste the time they did have. "We are good together. Do not allow tonight to change that."

"I need more, Tino."

"Then I will give you more." He was very good at that.

"I'm not talking about sex."

He turned her to face him and lowered his head so his lips hovered above hers. "Let's not talk at all."

Then he kissed her. He would show her that they were too right together to dismiss their relationship because it wasn't packaged in orange blossoms and meters of white tulle.

She fought her own response. He could feel the tension in her, knew she wanted to resist, but though she might want to, she was as much a slave to their mutual attraction as he. Her body knew where it belonged. In his arms.

But her brain was too active and she tore her lips from his. "No, Tino."

"Do not say no. Say rather, 'Make love to me, Tino.' This is what I wish to hear."

"We're supposed to be exclusive."

"We are."

"You were willing to have a blind date with another woman, Tino." She wrenched herself from his arms. "I cannot be okay with that."

"It was not a date."

She glared at him, but it was the light of betrayal in her eyes that cut him to the quick. "As good as."

"I did not consider it a date."

"But you knew your son and mother were matchmaking."

"I had no intention of being matched."

"But that's changed. You said so. You said you would do anything for Gio, even give him a second mother—*if she's Sicilian.*" The tone Faith spoke the last words with said how little she thought of his stance on the matter.

"I said I was considering it, not that I had decided to date other women. You are all the woman I want right now."

"And tomorrow?"

"And tomorrow."

"So, when does my sell-by date come into effect? Next week? Next month? Next year."

He wanted to grab her and hold on tight, but

he laid gentle hands on her shoulders instead. "You do not have a sell-by date. Our relationship is not cut-and-dried like that."

"I won't be with you if you're going to date other women," she repeated stubbornly.

"I would not ask you to."

"What does that mean, Tino?"

"It means you can trust me to be faithful while we are together. Just as I trust you."

Her eyes glistened suspiciously, sending shards of pain spiking through his gut. He did not want to see her cry. He kissed her, just once, oh so carefully, trying to put the tenderness and commitment—as limited as it might be—that he felt into the caress.

"Let me make love to you." He was pleading and he did not care.

They needed each other tonight, not empty beds where regrets and memories would haunt the hours that should be for sleep. Or making love.

"No more blind dates."

"It wasn't—"

But she shushed him with a finger to his lips. "It was. Or would have been. Don't do it again."

"You have my word." Then, because he could not help himself; because he needed it more than breathing or thinking or anything else, he once again kissed her.

He poured his passion and his fear out in that kiss, molding their lips together in a primordial dance.

At first she did not respond. She did not try to push him away, but she did not pull him closer, either. It was the only time in their relationship she had not fallen headfirst into passion with him.

She was still thinking.

He would fix that. Increasing the intensity of their kiss, he stormed her mouth, refusing to allow their mutual desire to remain a prisoner to circumstances that would not…could not… change. Bit by bit her instincts took over.

And once her brain caught up to her body, she melted into him, ending her resistance and giving him access to the interior of her mouth at the same time. She tasted like the coffee laced heavily with rich cream and sweet sugar she had drunk after dinner. It was a flavor he had come to associate only with her.

He drank his own coffee black unless he wanted an erection tenting his slacks—something that was more than inconvenient during his business day, but could be downright embarrassing. This, what they had, was beyond good. It was fantastic, and she *would* not end it. He could not let her.

Tonight, he would remind her how well he knew her body, what he alone could do to it, how much pleasure *he* could give her. Her husband had not elicited those sensations in her, or she would not have acted so shocked by each new one when Tino and Faith had first begun their affair.

She had been almost virginal, many of her reactions belying the existence of previous lovers, much less a husband.

He refused to dwell on the sense of alarm he felt realizing the extent of his ignorance about her life. She'd been his son's art teacher since before they met a year ago, and she had known his mother even longer. Yet Tino had been totally unaware of those facts. As unknowing as he had been about the reality of Faith's widowhood.

How had her husband died? She'd loved him, thought he was a *special* man.

A primal need to erase memories of the other male from her drove Tino to deepen the kiss even further.

Faith made a soft sound against his lips. He loved kissing her. Had from the very first. She was more responsive to his lips claiming hers than any woman he had ever known. And she was far from shyly submissive. She gave as good as she got, with a passion that turned him inside out.

Damn. He wanted her.

But not out here where someone might see what should be entirely private between two people. The temptation to once again make her his, right here under the stars, was strong however. He fought it, sweeping her up into his arms and carrying her inside.

He went directly to his room, no thought of taking Faith anywhere else even entering his mind. This was *his* bedroom. *His* bed. And for now at least, she was his woman.

The huge four-poster with wooden canopy

had been used by his family for generations. Though the mattress and box springs were new—a pillow-top with extra coils imported from America on his younger brother's recommendation. It had been a good piece of advice, for more than one reason.

Not only was it incredibly comfortable, but giving up the mattress and even the bed linens he had shared with his wife had been instrumental in Tino finally being able to sleep in his own suite once again.

Pulling back the coverlet, he then laid Faith onto the bed.

She looked around the room, her expression going from curious to surprised. "This is your room."

He locked the door and returned to the bed, unbuttoning his shirt as he went. "Where else would I take you?"

"I don't know." She licked her lips, her focus on his chest as he peeled the shirt from his body. "You're such an incredibly sexy man, you know?"

"You have mentioned believing so before."

She laughed, the sound husky and warm. "I

meant it then and I mean it now. I love looking at you."

"I thought it was men who were supposed to be the visual sex."

"Maybe." She shrugged, kicking her sandals off. "Maybe if all women had such yummy eye candy to look at, we'd be considered the visual sex, too."

"So, I am eye candy?"

She licked her lips as if tasting something really sweet and nodded.

His sex jolted at memories of what it felt like to be partaken of by that delectable little tongue. "I think you are a minx."

"You think?"

"I know."

She gave him a saucy wink and stretched her body, putting her curves on sensual display.

He shook his head but knew he had no hope of clearing it. He'd been here before with this woman, so filled with desire that everything else was just a gray fog around them. He unzipped his slacks, hissing as the parting fabric made way for his steel-hard manhood.

This woman affected him like no other.

"I love it when you make that sound."

"You are the only one who has ever heard it." With his admission, he stripped off the remainder of his clothes—the need to deflect automatic.

"Really?" she asked, nevertheless.

"Yes." He joined her on the bed, on all fours above her. "I want you naked."

She brushed her hand down his flank. "I like naked."

He could no more suppress the growl her touch evoked than he could the need to return it. He brought their mouths together again as he reached down and caressed her through the silk of her dress. All evening he had wanted to do this, to feel the curves he knew intimately through the thin fabric. Regardless of how surreal the night had been, his desire for her was as strong as always, building with each minute he was in her company.

She moaned into the kiss, arching into his touch, begging silently for more.

And more was what he was an expert at giving her. He would remind her of that. Show her that each time could be better than the last.

He continued the strokes along her breasts, the dip of her waist and bow of her hips. Over and over again, he touched the places on her body that he knew drove her wild.

Her hands were busy, too, skimming along his heated skin, kneading his chest, but best of all was when she grabbed him—her fingers digging into his shoulders with white-knuckle intensity. When she got to this point—where she could no longer concentrate on pleasuring him—he knew she was past thought. Past control.

Exactly where he wanted her to be.

CHAPTER FOUR

IT WAS time to take her clothes off. He did, using the opportunity to tease and tantalize her further. But revealing her peaches-and-cream body was a double-edged sword. The light smattering of freckles over her shoulders and upper breasts were his downfall. She had none on her face, so the cinnamon dots felt secret—private—for him alone. A special knowledge shared just between them. He was tempted to count them—with kisses—every time he got her disrobed.

This time was no different.

The allure of her body for him never diminished.

He traced the light dots on her skin. "You are so beautiful."

"You've got an unnatural affection for my

freckles." It might be a full sentence, but the way she said it, breathless with pauses between words, told him that she was no more in possession of her faculties than she had been a moment before.

"You think?" he asked against her silken skin, tasting the brown sugar dots that his mind told him could not be sweet but his tongue told him they were. But then, everything about her was sweet.

Dangerously so.

Her only answer was a moan as his lips trailed the natural path to one pebbled nipple. She shuddered beneath him, her body translating her every feeling with sexy clarity. She loved nipple play and he loved tasting and touching the turgid buds.

He delicately licked the very tip, then circled the peak with his tongue, moving slowly to lave her aureole despite the need riding him hard enough to make him ache. He refused to rush this. He had something to prove to her.

He kept at it until even the act of huffing a warm breath over her sensitized skin made her tremble and whimper. Then he moved to minister in the same way to its twin.

"What are you doing? Tormenting me?" she cried out as he sucked her nipple gently into his mouth.

He lifted his head and met peacock blue eyes glazed with pleasure. "I am giving you more."

"I don't want more. I want you in me." Then she bit her lip as if realizing what she'd said.

"Trust me, this—" he carefully slid two fingers into her superbly lubricated, swollen channel "—this is where I wish to be also, but only when I have given you *more*." He thrust with his fingers, hitting that interior bundle of nerves some women referred to as their G-spot.

She cried out, the sound adding to his own arousal, making it harder to wait, but he would.

Tonight would be spectacular.

He continued to massage her as he leaned down and once again claimed her mouth as his. Her return kisses were desperate and filled with the feminine fire he found so irresistible.

Her walls clenched around his fingers as he moved them in and out, stimulating her G-spot with each slow stroke. She undulated, her body straining toward him and moving with those tiny, involuntary jerks that enhanced her pleasure.

He could feel her need to climax rolling off her in palpable waves of sexual energy. Her little whimpers against his lips were an inarticulate form of begging he'd become addicted to their first time together.

His Faith did not play mind games or try to hide her physical needs or desires. She expressed them in a dozen different ways, all of which turned him on. Sex with this woman was volcanically hot, but it was also honest. She amazed and delighted him.

Now it was his turn.

He brushed her clitoris with his thumb, just a light movement back and forth...back and forth, but that was all she needed. Launching upward with her pelvis, she convulsed around his fingers. Her sharp little teeth bit into his lower lip as she made a keening sound in her throat, telling him without words that this was exactly what he wanted it to be.

More.

He kissed her through the orgasm, helping

her to come down, but not too far. He was not done with her yet. Not nearly.

When her breathing was less ragged, he gently lifted her legs so they draped over his forearms and he used the position to spread her thighs until she was completely open to his gaze. Her entire body was still flushed from her climax, a beautiful rose red that he could not wait to spear with his own throbbing and as yet unsatisfied flesh. Diamond hard, her nipples poked straight up, pleading for his touch. A soft sheen of perspiration coated her upper chest, attesting to the level of pleasure she had already received.

He started to speak and had to clear his throat.

She smiled at him and the words came out in a masculine growl he wasn't in any way ashamed of. "You are so incredibly beautiful like this."

"Sated from your lovemaking?"

"You are not sated." He tipped his pelvis, brushing her entrance with the tip of his penis, eliciting a second keening sound from her. He smiled. "You still need me."

Something flashed in her eyes, something he

could not quite read but that looked a lot like vulnerability. "Yes."

"I need you as well."

"I know." But the words came out sounding bleak.

He did not like it. There was no place for melancholy in their bed.

"You are not my mistress." He didn't know why he said it, but he felt compelled.

Her eyes widened. "What?"

"You are not my mistress. You are *amore mio* and my friend."

"Yes." The smile she gave him was still tinged with sadness, but a glimmer of hope shone in her gaze.

Why it should matter to him that it was there, that he would even desire such a thing, considering what it implied from her earlier words, he did not know. But illogical as it might be, he was glad.

"I am going to give you more now, *carina*. Are you ready for me?"

She nodded, her breath coming out in little pants, but her body did not tense in his hold. She trusted him completely. Amazing. Although she had climaxed, her body was ready for *more*. Ready for *him*.

He pressed forward, allowing the head of his granite-hard penis to brush her opening again, but did not go in, teasing them both. Her lips curved in a familiar smile as she seemed to simply melt against the bed, waiting on him with a sexy expectation he adored. It said she knew he would take care of her wants.

He thrust his hips, allowing his length to slide along her slick folds. It felt so good—so perfect—he groaned, the sound reverberating deep in his chest. With her, he was primal man. "You are so wet."

"You are so earthy, Tino. No one would expect it." Using her lower back muscles, she lifted herself and increased the stimulation, showing the uninhibited aspect of her own nature.

"Only you get to see this side of me." That had to count for something.

"I better be the only one, mister."

He laughed softly as he allowed his thickened member to enter her. "You are like hot silk. I feel like I am going to lose my mind every time I enter you."

"I lost mine a long time ago." She pressed her head back into the pillow, her eyelids going half-mast.

He smiled and shook his head as he moved forward with rocking motions that made it possible for her to take his entire length. He was long and thick, and that had overwhelmed more than one lover. His and Maura's intimacy had been loving and passionate, but nothing like what it was like with Faith.

Maura had never been as comfortable exposing her desire, which was to be expected as she had been raised in the very sheltered environment of a traditional Sicilian household. But he adored that element of Faith's lovemaking. The way his current lover not only *could* take his full length, but *craved* it was something a man like him could and would never take for granted.

He could not help rejoicing in the amount of belief in him that Faith expressed every time they came together.

"You never flinch from me." The wonder that laced his voice embarrassed him a little, but like so many things with this woman—was an uncontrollable response.

In so many ways she was dangerous to him, but he continued to play Russian Roulette with his emotions—risking the promises he had made to his dead wife. His brain told him he should get out before he got in too deep, but everything inside him rebelled at the idea.

"Why would I?" Her brows wrinkled in genuine confusion. "We are a perfect fit."

Perfect only because she relaxed so well for him—for she was tight. Oh, so damn tight. *"So, perfect."*

"Mmmm…" She licked her lips. "You're big, but it's *good*, Tino."

"It is better than good."

"Yessss…" she hissed as he finally sheathed himself to the hilt in her fantastic heat.

He tucked her legs around his hips. "I need to kiss you."

"Please, Tino." She was straining toward him even as he brought their mouths together.

Nothing had ever felt so good.

The part of his brain where guilt resided rejected that thought even as he set a steady, slow rhythm. Kissing, their bodies moved together in a motion filled with tenderness he did not want to examine.

He could feel her desire building as was his. He refused to go over, no matter how much his body clamored for the ultimate release. He was determined to bring her to another shattering peak. Her second climax would be more intense than the first.

It would be *more*.

Of its own volition, his pelvis swiveled on each downward thrust, as if his body had been trained to pleasure this woman exactly as she needed. Pavlov's response. Her pleasure gave him intense satisfaction and pleasure, therefore he did all that he could to bring out every little gasp, each sweet moan, every tightening of her muscles, each shudder she could not control.

Suddenly they were both coming together, his own orgasm taking him over before he could even hope to stop it.

But he did not want to as she contracted around him, her peak lasting seconds that turned into minutes while his body vibrated with matching sensation until his muscles felt like they would collapse.

Their mouths separated, allowing each of them to take in gasps of air and he collapsed, managing only to deflect part of his weight to the side, but maintaining skin contact. From past experience, he knew she preferred that. Thank the Holy Mother because he could not have moved if he tried.

"Thank you."

"No, *cara,* thank you."

She made another sound, but he knew she would slide into sleep soon. People said men fell asleep after sex, but he rarely did. His little American lover, however, experienced orgasm as some kind of somnolence button. He did not mind. He looked forward to these moments when he could cuddle her without having to put up his macho facade.

But tonight he did something he never did. Or at least had not until their last time together in his apartment in Marsala. He let his body relax in preparation for sleep.

Although Giosue woke early, Valentino always woke even earlier. He was not worried about being caught with her. Besides, there just seemed to be something so cold about kicking her out of his bed after such an intense experience. It had been getting harder and harder to do so lately, anyway.

He was going to have to get a handle on this softening of his relationship rules, but not tonight. He wanted to sleep, for just a little while, holding Faith.

Gio would never know and therefore could not be hurt by it. He would no doubt sleep even later than he normally did on a Saturday morning. Valentino had allowed his son to stay up later than usual because of their guest.

Their *guest*.

His lover.

He mentally shook his head at that. He would never have guessed that she was so ingrained in the life of his family. He still was not sure how he felt about that, but he wasn't going to dwell on it tonight. Tomorrow was soon enough to try to figure out how the woman who had shared his bed for almost a year was such an enigma to him.

Just as it would be soon enough to reinstate his necessary rules for the women who shared his bed. Or perhaps he should reconsider those rules for Faith. At least a little.

After all, she was more than a mere bed partner.

She was his friend.

A friend he apparently knew less about than any of his business rivals. And he trusted her enough to share an intimate side of his life.

For the second time ever, Faith woke in the arms of her lover.

Tino had allowed her to *sleep in his bed? In his family home?*

Maybe he really had given her *more* last night.

Or had that move been an unconscious one? It didn't really matter if he had considered it, or acted on instinct—it had to mean something.

Just as his promise not to go searching for that perfect Sicilian paragon right away meant something. Gio was Tino's heart, but the dedicated father had still reaffirmed his commitment not to date other women while he and Faith were together.

She'd thought her heart was being ripped right out of her chest when he said he thought Gio might need a new mother, but that mother could not be Faith. She'd been angry and hurt and scared and a lot of other emotions that confused her because she couldn't be sure if they were genuine or induced by the pregnancy hormones rampaging through her body.

The two pregnancies she'd had before had sparked serious inner upheavals as well. She and Tay would have argued constantly if he hadn't taken her hormone-driven insecurities in his stride. Would Tino have the same patience? Did she want him to? There had been instances when Tay's tolerance had felt more patronizing than understanding.

Right now she felt she was out of control when it came to her feelings and she didn't enjoy the experience. There had been times the night before she'd been sorely tempted to sock

Tino good and hard, but then the pendulum that was her emotions had swung to needing the re-assurance that sex provided.

She didn't think Tino was any surer of his feelings than she was. Because in the same con-versation he'd spoken of getting Gio a Sicilian mother, he'd also spoken of not wanting to end things with Faith. He knew she wouldn't be any man's mistress.

Early in their acquaintance, she'd made sure he was aware of how she felt about those kinds of double standards.

Their intimacy last night had been awesome, she couldn't deny it. She'd felt more connected to Tino than ever before. He'd been so intent on giving her pleasure, but more than that, he'd given her something of himself. It was in the way he'd moved inside her, with an undisputable tender-ness that brought tears to her eyes just before they'd found the ultimate pleasure *together.*

As much as she hated to, she forced herself to slide from his embrace. Even if she thought Tino could handle it, she did not want to be caught in his bed by anyone in his household, but especially by Gio. She loved the little boy too much to spring such a relationship on him without some sort of leading up to it.

He might be playing matchmaker, but that didn't mean he was ready for the reality of his father having a lover, a woman who had taken his mother's place in the huge four-poster bed. She still could not believe they had made love in his bedroom. That not only had he initiated the lovemaking, but *he* had *carried* her in here.

She took a quick shower in his en suite, halting midstep on the way out by the sight of the statue on his dresser. It was of a faceless woman, her arms outstretched to a man holding a baby boy. The man was faceless and so was the baby, but she knew it was male.

How could she not? She'd done the statue. The original, complete with perfect replicas of her own face and that of Taylish holding a little boy whose features were an amalgam of both of them resided in her studio at home.

"My mother bought it for me."

That didn't surprise Faith. Nor did the fact that Tino was awake. He slept too lightly not to have woken to the shower running. "Do you like it?"

"Very much. It reminds me of when Maura was alive."

"Oh." Of course…there was nothing in this statue to show the deep sorrow that etched her face in the original.

"It is as if she has her arms open, welcoming Gio and myself into them."

"Or as if she's letting you go." That's what she'd titled the first one she'd done, but when she created another faceless rendition, she'd simply called it *Family*.

"Is that wishful thinking?" Tino asked, an edge to his voice.

She turned to face him. "What do you mean?"

"Are you hoping my wife has finally let me go so that I might claim someone new in her place?" There was nothing to give away what he was thinking in his face.

It didn't matter. The only course open to her—especially now—was honesty. "If I say yes?"

"I will remind you that if I ever do remarry it will be to a Sicilian woman, someone who can give Gio that little part of his mother at the very least." Pain flashed in his eyes, quickly followed by guilt and then both were gone, leaving only the stoic expression behind.

Promise not to date others notwithstanding, she could really have done without that reminder. The knowledge he was still so adamant about not marrying her hurt. Badly. And she was absolutely certain that pain was not a hormones-gone-wild-induced emotion.

"Why did you let me sleep here last night?" she had to ask as she fought against showing the pain his words had caused.

"I fell asleep."

"You never just fall asleep."

"There is a first time for everything."

So it had been subconscious. She'd wondered and now she knew. He didn't know why he'd brought her to his bed in his family home. And honestly? That didn't matter right now. What did matter was that he regretted it. That much was obvious. Anything else he might be feeling was hidden behind the enigmatic mask he wore.

And she should not be surprised.

She was the first woman to share that bed since the death of his wife. As hard as his regret was for her to bear, the situation was equally difficult for him. Only in a different way.

She'd had her own moments of letting go in the years since Taylish and their unborn son had died. She knew how wrenching they could be. Regardless of her own feelings right now, she could not ignore the pain twisting inside Tino. It was not in her nature to do so, but beyond that—she loved him.

She caressed the statue. It was a beautiful piece. One of her favorites. The one in her studio expressed and brought a measure of peace for an emotional agony she had been unable to give voice to. No one had been there to hear.

She would be there for Tino now, if he wanted her to be. "Tino—"

"I won't be able to see you again until my parents return." The words were clipped, hard.

"I understand." She really did.

He stood there, silent, as if he expected her to say something else.

"It's all right, Tino." She gave one last lingering glance at the statue and then began
dressing.

He flinched, as if those were not the words he
wanted or expected to hear. "I *will* see you then?"

She paused in the act of slipping on her
sandals. "Of course."

"Good." He nodded, looking at a loss. So different from the typical Tino—business tycoon
and suave but distant lover.

When she was done dressing she stopped in
front of him and leaned up to kiss his cheek. "It
really is going to be all right." Letting go was a
necessary part of grief.

The fact that Tino was doing so, even if only
on a subconscious level, gave her hope.

"No doubt."

"It isn't easy for any of us."

"What do you mean?" he asked, edgy again.
Or still. He hadn't relaxed since she came out
of the bathroom.

"Letting go."

"I have nothing to let go of."

She didn't argue. There would be no point.

And it would only make him more determined to prove himself right. He had enough to overcome in moving forward, without adding another dose of his stubborn will to the mix.

"I'll see you when your parents return from Naples."

Valentino swore and slammed his hand down beside the statue Faith had admired. His wife letting him go? He did not think so.

Maura would be in his heart forever. He had promised.

The memory was as visceral today as it had been an hour after it happened.

His beautiful young wife had started off not feeling well that morning. He'd had the temerity to hope it meant she was pregnant again.

But that had not been the case.

Ignorant of the tragedy to come, he'd flown out of country for a business meeting in Greece with hope in his heart of increasing his family. He remembered that while his wife's body betrayed her and she slipped further away from him, he had spent the day smiling more than usual, feeling on top of the world. And then his world had come crashing down.

His meeting had been a success, opening the doors for the major expansion of the Grisafi family interests. He would exchange that success and all that had come later for one more lucid day with the mother of his son.

Valentino's mother had called him just before he boarded the jet for home. Papa had taken Maura to the hospital because she had passed out walking up the stairs. By the time Valentino had reached the hospital, his wife was in a coma.

Petrified for the first time in his life, sweating through his expensive shirt, he'd rushed into the room. Maura had been so damn pale and completely motionless. He'd taken her lifeless hand, his heart ceasing at its coolness. He had begged her to wake up, to speak to him, to squeeze his hand—anything.

But nothing. Not then. Not later. No fluttering eyelids. No half-formed words. No goodbyes. Absolutely nothing.

The only sounds had come from him—his desperate pleas and constant talking until his voice was no more than a horse whisper in hopes of sparking a connection to her shut-down brain—and from the machines hooked up to her. Machines and medications that had been unsuccessful at saving her life.

Her first discernable diabetic attack had been her last. Nothing the doctors did brought her blood sugars under control and she died without coming out of the coma.

He'd spent every minute with her, but it had done no good. And when she'd gone into cardiac arrest, the doctors had called security to force him from the room. He'd been in another country when she fell into the coma and out in the hall when she let go of life.

The doctors said her reaction to the disease was extremely rare. But not rare enough, was it? His wife, the mother of his child was dead and nothing would ever change that.

He would never forget the rage, the grief and the utter helplessness he felt holding his small son in his arms as they said goodbye to her. He had promised then, standing over her grave, holding their sobbing son who just wanted his mama. Valentino had promised he would never stop loving her, that he would never replace her in his heart.

Valentino Grisafi had never broken a promise and he wasn't about to start now.

This thing with Faith had to get back on track, or it had to end.

There simply was no other option. No matter what he might want or think he needed.

CHAPTER FIVE

TRUE to his word, Faith did not see Tino again while Agata and Rocco were in Naples. There were no more phone calls, either.

She didn't expect there to be.

Tino wasn't going to accept the change in their relationship gracefully. If he accepted it at all. She had to believe he would though.

Especially after allowing him to make love to her that night. Not that she'd had a lot of choice. Once he set his course on seduction, she was a goner. She loved him. *Needed him*. While that truth scared her to death, she didn't try to deny it. Self-deception was not something she indulged in. She'd accepted the physical intimacy because it substituted for the emotional connection she craved after learning she carried his baby. And sometimes, when he made love to her, she actually felt loved by him—if only for that short while.

It was that simple. And that complicated.

But maybe it was on the way to something better…something truly *more*.

He had initiated the shift in their relationship in the first place. Initially, sleeping all night with her in his apartment in Marsala, and then making love to her in his family home. That reality mitigated her fears for their future, although it did not completely rid her of them.

He might not want to admit it, but he was already thinking about her in broader terms than simply his "current convenient partner." They'd been exclusive from the very beginning—something they had both insisted on. Add that to how well she fit with his family and their friendship and they had a strong basis for a lasting relationship. The fact that she loved him would only make it easier to raise a family with him.

Even if he never came to love her as he'd loved Maura, it would be enough to be his wife and mother of his children. She had never expected to have this much claim to family again. She certainly did not expect it all.

Not after everything she had lost.

Besides, she'd never loved Taylish like she loved Tino, but *he'd* been happy in their marriage. Content to have her loving commitment if not her passion.

There were times she knew he had wanted more, but he'd never regretted their marriage. Only leaving it in death. He'd told her so, just before breathing his last.

But she didn't want to remember that day. It belonged in her past—along with the two families she'd lost. The only real families she'd ever had. Until now.

Her current hopes and dreams were reflected in the series of joy-filled family centric sculptures she did over the next week.

Agata called her when the older couple returned from the continent. Faith did not tell her about having dinner with Tino and Giosue, leaving that bit of information for them to reveal. She also avoided having Agata come to her studio the following week. She did not want Tino's mother to see the revealing pieces of art before Faith had a chance to tell him of his impending fatherhood.

Every day that went by and she did not hear from him, she missed him more. She wanted to share the miracle of her pregnancy with him, but it was important to give him space. He had to come to terms on his own with the new parameters of their relationship.

However, when the silence between them stretched a week beyond his parents' return, she called him. Only to discover he'd had to fly to New York to meet with his brother and a potential client. She tried his cell phone, but the call went straight to voice mail. After that had happened a couple of times, once very late in the evening, she figured out he was avoiding her with diligence.

It bothered her, feeling a lot like rejection. She clung to the knowledge that if he wanted to break it off with her, he would do so definitively. He would not simply begin avoiding her like an adolescent. No, he was just struggling with the changes between them more than she'd anticipated.

It made her nervous about how he might react to the news of her pregnancy. Thankfully, he was as Sicilian as a man could get. Some might think that meant unreconstructed male, but she knew that for Tino that translated into an all-out love for family and children especially. He might not be thrilled about her new role in his life, but he would be happy about the baby. Being the traditional Sicilian that he was, it would never occur to him to seek a relationship with the child that excluded her.

Thank goodness.

His desire to marry a Sicilian woman if he ever did remarry worried her a little, but he would just have to buck up and deal with it like a grown-up. It wasn't as if he objected to her personally. He liked her as much outside the bedroom as in it. She was sure of it. Even at his apartment they did not spend all their time in bed together.

And when they were in bed, they didn't only have sex. They talked. Not about anything personal, but about politics, faith, what they thought of the latest news, his business—the types of things you didn't talk about with a bare acquaintance.

He might know much about her art career, but he knew her stance on environmentalism, government deficits, latch-key children and his desire to dominate his own corner of the upscale wine market.

Right now, though, he had to adjust to the fact that she was a part of his family's life and a bigger part of his than he had intended when they first got together.

In the meantime, she agreed to join Agata for lunch at the Vineyard.

A day earlier than he had told his family to expect him, Valentino pulled his car into his spot in the newer multicar garage he'd had built to the side of the house when he married Maura. So she could keep her car parked inside for her comfort. She'd teased him about spoiling her, but it had been so easy to do. His dead wife had been a very sweet woman.

Much like Faith.

He sighed at the thought, frustrated with himself.

The trip to New York had been longer than he wanted or expected, though it had one side benefit. It had made it easier to distance himself from Faith. Though forwarding her calls directly to voice mail had taken a larger measure of self-control than he would have expected. Much larger.

Which only went to show that he had to become serious about getting their relationship back on track.

Or he would have to let her go, and that was not something he wanted to do.

The craving he felt to hear her voice filled him with anger at himself along with a sense of helplessness he refused to give in to. He had been fighting the urge to sleep all night with her since the beginning. Never before had he been tempted not to be home in the morning for his son to wake up to because of a woman. He'd known giving in would come with a cost, but he had not expected it to be his sanity.

It had felt right taking her to his bed in the family home. Too right. Now he questioned his intelligence in doing so. For that insanely stupid choice had come at an emotional cost, as well, one he had no right to pay.

If he were a truly honorable man, he would let her go completely. He'd told himself so over and over again while in New York. What did it say for his inner strength that he could not do it?

Certainly it was nothing to be proud of.

Physically distancing himself from her was not the same as regrouped emotions, he had learned. His need to see her grew with each day even as he fought it. He might have won, but he hungered for not only the sound of her voice, but the shiver of her laughter and the feel of her skin. He was like a drug addict shaking for his next fix.

It would be a couple of days at least before he could go to her, too. Agonizing days if those in New York were anything to go by. But Gio had missed his papa and had to be Valentino's first consideration.

Of course, if he left when his son was sleeping, Gio would be missing nothing.

The thought derailed from its already shaky tracks as he recognized the melodious laughter mingled with his mother's voice coming from the terrace. He stood frozen, uncharacteristically unsure of what to do. No doubts about what he *wanted* to do. He wanted to see Faith. But what *should* he do?

His decision was taken from him by his mother's voice. "Valentino, *figlio mio,* is that you?"

"*Si,* Mama. It is me."

"Come out here."

He had no choice but to obey. He might be thirty years old, but a Sicilian man knew better than to dismiss a direct command from his mother. It would hurt her and cause her distress. Hurting those he loved was something he avoided at all costs. Even when it was his peace of mind at stake, like now.

Walking out onto the terrace, he found not only his mother and Faith, but his father and Giosue as well.

His son jumped up from where he'd been dangling his feet in the water beside Faith and came running full tilt at Valentino. "Papa, Papa…you are home!"

"*Si,* I am home and glad to be here." He swung his son high into his arms and hugged the wiggling, eight-year-old body to his.

"I missed you, Papa. *Zio* Calogero should not call you to New York."

"Sometimes it is necessary, *cucciola*. You know this."

His son ducked his head. "Papa! Do not call me that. It is a name for little boys, but I am big. I am eight!"

"Ah, but a man's son is always his little one," Rocco Grisafi said as he came and hugged both Valentino and Giosue. "Welcome home, *piccolo,*" his father said, emphasizing his point with a humorous glint in eyes the same color as Valentino's.

It had been decades since his father had last called him that and Valentino laughed.

Giosue giggled. "Papa is bigger than you Nonno, how can he be your little one?"

Valentino's father, who was in fact a head shorter than he, winked at his grandson. "It is not about size, it is about age, and I will always be older, no?"

"That's right," Valentino agreed. "And I will always be older than you," he said as he tickled his swimsuit-clad son.

Giosue screeched with laughter and squirmed down, running to the pool and jumping in, his head immediately coming up out of the water. "You can't get me now, Papa."

"You think I cannot?"

"I know it. Nonna would be mad if you got your business clothes wet."

That made everyone laugh, including Faith, drawing Valentino's attention like a bee to a rose. *Damn, damn, damn.* She was beautiful, wearing a bright green top and matching pair of Capri pants she had rolled up above her knees so she could dangle her feet in the water of the pool. Her gorgeous red hair fell loose around her shoulders and her sandals were nowhere to be seen.

Even his mother's hug and greeting got only a portion of his attention as the rest of him strained toward the woman he wanted to take into his arms and kiss the daylights out of.

"So, I hear from my grandson that you and my

dear friend are well acquainted already," his mother said, finally garnering his whole focus.

Well versed in how his mother's mind worked, he immediately went hyperalert to any nuance and ultracautious in his own reactions. She was on a kick to get him married and fathering more grandbabies for her. His argument that it was time for Calogero to do his duty by the family was met with deaf ears.

His mother wanted more grandchildren from Valentino. Full stop. Period.

And now she'd discovered he was friends with Faith.

He had to be very careful here. If his mother even got a hint of the intimate nature of his relationship with Faith, Agata Grisafi would have her oldest son married off before he could get a word in edgewise. "We'd met before, yes."

"You'd met? I am sure your son said you were friends," his mother chided with a gleam in her eyes, confirming Valentino's worst fears.

He simply shrugged, confirming nothing. Denying nothing. Sometimes that was the only way to deal with his mother and her machinations. Deflection wasn't a bad tactic, either, when he could get away with it.

He'd long ago acknowledged he never wanted to face his mother across a boardroom table. She made his toughest clients and strongest competition look like amateurs.

"More interesting to me is your friendship with her," he said. "You rarely mention Faith."

"You are joking me, my son. I talk about my dear friend TK all of the time."

"Yes, but what has that to do with Faith?"

His mother's eyes widened and she flicked a glance to the woman in question. Faith was not looking at them, but her shoulders were stiff with unmistakable tension. This grilling had to be causing her stress as well.

"You are *not* good friends, are you?" his mother asked, in a tone that said she no longer had any doubts about the superficial nature of their relationship.

Relieved, but unsure what had convinced her, he simply said, "We know each other."

"Not very well."

He shrugged again, but had a strong urge to

deny what felt like an accusation. Though the words had been spoken in his mother's normal voice, his own emotions convicted him.

Mama shrugged, looking smug, her expression that of a woman who knew what he did not. "Faith Williams is TK."

"Your artist friend?" he asked in genuine shock. "I thought he was a man!"

"No, she is very much a female, as you can see." The laughter lacing his mother's voice did not faze him.

The memory of Faith saying maybe the woman in the statue on his dresser was letting go did. *She* was the artist of that particular piece of art. When she'd made the comment, she could have been hinting, but more likely she was exposing the true inspiration behind the figure.

Which meant what? That she had a son? "You did not tell me you had a child," he said to her.

She stood up and faced him. "If you will recall, the *father* is holding the child," she said, proving once again that their thoughts traveled similar paths.

"What is that supposed to signify?"

"Figure it out for yourself, Tino. Or better yet, ask your mother. Agata understands far more than you do and knows me much better."

He couldn't believe she was being so argumentative in front of his family. His mother was bound to realize there was more between them than a casual friendship if Faith kept this up. Hell, if he had to explain what they were talking about, things would get dicey. The statue was in his bedroom, after all. How could he explain Faith—his not so good friend— seeing it?

"It's not important," he said, in an attempt to put sand on the fire of his mother's curiosity.

"No, I don't suppose it is." Faith turned to his mother and gave her a strained smile. "It's time for me to be going."

"But I thought you would stay for dinner."

"Yes, do not let my arrival change your plans." He wanted to see Faith, even if it meant being judicious under the watchful eye of his family.

He knew it was not the smartest attitude to take. He was supposed to be cooling down their relationship, but seeing her brought into sharp relief just how hard that had been over the past weeks. How much he had *missed* her.

"I feel the need to create." She hugged his mother. "You know how it is for me when I have a fit of inspiration. You are not offended, are you?"

"Will you let me see the results of this inspiration?" Agata asked. "I am still waiting to see the pieces you made while Rocco and I were in Naples."

Faith's hand dropped to her stomach, like she was nervous. "I'll let you see them all eventually. You know that."

"You promise? I know how you artists are. Especially you. If you think a piece is not up to standards, you will pound it back into clay."

That strained smile crossed Faith's beautiful features again. "I can't promise to keep something I hate, but you should be used to that by now."

His mother gave a long-suffering sigh, but she hugged Faith warmly. "I am. You cannot blame me for trying, though. You have spoiled me, allowing me access to your work before you do others."

Faith's laugh was even more strained than her smile. "You are my friend." Even though he was wet from the pool, she hugged Giosue goodbye, as well. "I will see you next week in school."

Her leave-taking of his father was the usual kisses on both cheeks. But she simply nodded at Tino before turning to go. Though it fit in with the facade of casual friendship he had tried to create, he felt the slight like a blow to his midsection.

He understood being careful in front of his parents, but this went beyond that. Had it been deliberate? Or was she simply doing her part to allay suspicion? Unfortunately, he could not ask her, nor could he request a more warm goodbye without looking suspect himself. They would have to talk about how to act in front of his family, as it was clear that was going to be an issue in the future. He was only surprised it had taken so long for the matter to arise, now that he knew how close she was to his mother and son.

That was secondary as he watched Faith walk away, and he had to fight everything in himself not to go after her.

"And you worried your mother was developing a *tendre* for TK," his father said with a big, amused laugh.

"Never say so!" His mother shook her head. "Sometimes, my son, you are singularly obtuse."

"But he is good at business," Giosue piped in, as if trying to stand up for his deficient father and not knowing exactly what to say.

Apparently everyone else in his family knew Faith's life more intimately than he did.

He was determined to rectify that ignorance. Starting now. "Mama, what did she mean by saying that the father was holding the baby in my statue?"

It was one of the reasons he loved the piece so much. It showed the father having a tender moment with his child as well as his wife.

His mother's pause before answering gave him time to realize what a monumentally stupid question that had been to ask. He had just gotten through admonishing himself regarding this very topic and here he was drawing attention to it.

No doubt about it. Faith Williams messed up

his equilibrium and made mush of his usually superior brain function.

There was nothing wrong with the way his mother's brain was working, however. "Do you mean the statue that I bought you? The one that you keep on the bureau in your *bedroom,* Valentino?" she asked delicately like a cat licking at cream.

"Yes, that is the one," he said with as much insouciance as he could muster under his mother's gimlet stare.

He offered no explanation and, surprisingly enough, she did not demand he do so. He could read the speculation in her eyes as easily as a first-year primer.

She looked down at her hands as if examining her manicure, which was incidentally perfect as usual, before looking back at him. "I'm not sure that is something she would care for me to share with you."

He wasn't about to be deterred after the huge gaffe he'd committed to get the information. "Mama," he said with exasperation. "She told me to ask you."

"*Si,* well, I suppose. You know she lost her husband to a car accident six years ago?"

"I know she is a widow, yes."

"She lost her child in the same accident."

"How horrible." It had nearly destroyed him to lose Maura; if he had lost Giosue as well, he did not know how he would have stood it.

"Just so." Mama reached out and hugged her wet grandson to her. "She sells her artwork under TK as a tribute to them. Her husband's name was Taylish and her son would have been named Kaden."

"Would have been?"

"She was pregnant. And from what she said, that was something of a minor miracle. Her life has not been an easy one. She was left an orphan by her mother's death years earlier. She never knew her father—or even who he was, I believe."

"Life has enough pain to make joy all the sweeter," his father said with the same pragmatism he spoke the well-used Sicilian proverb, *cu' avi 'nna bona vigna avi pani, vinu e linga.*

He who owns a good vineyard has bread, wine and wood.

The Sicilian people were a practical lot. The fatalism of their cultural thinking reflected in the fact that Sicilian vernacular had no future tense. Just past and present.

Regardless of his pragmatic heritage, Valentino found it almost debilitatingly painful to discover that his happy-go-lucky Faith had such a sorrow-filled past. Her optimistic nature was one of the things he found most attractive about her. She made him feel good just being around.

To discover that her attitude was in spite of past agonies, not because she had never had any, was so startling as to leave him speechless.

"I think Signora Guglielmo wanted to be a mama very much," Giosue said. "She loves all the children at school, even the bratty ones."

His son's observation made Valentino chuckle even as it made him sad for the woman who had to find an outlet for her nurturing nature with other people's children.

He remembered her once telling him that she believed she was not meant to have a family. He had assumed that meant she thought she was not cut out to be a mother. He had not minded knowing that at all, as it assured him she would not expect marriage and children someday down the road. Now he saw a far more disturbing meaning behind the words.

When Faith had said she wanted more from him, she truly had meant *more*. She wanted what she had thought she could not have. A family.

And the only way he could give it to her was to break a promise that for him was sacred.

It was not an option.

But neither was letting her go so she could find that with someone else.

CHAPTER SIX

FAITH drove like an automaton toward Pizzolato. *They'd met? They knew each other?*

Each word Tino had used to answer his mother's innocent questions had driven into her heart with the precision of an assassin's dagger. And the wounds were still raw and bleeding. As they would be for a very long time.

How could he dismiss her as if she meant *nothing* to him?

But she had the answer to that, an answer she wanted to ignore, to pretend no knowledge of for the sake of her lacerated heart. She only wished she could do it—that she could lie to herself as easily as she had deluded herself into believing things were changing between them.

He could dismiss her as someone of no importance in his life because that was exactly what she was. She was his *convenient sex partner.* Nothing more. Friends? When it was convenient for him to think so, but that clearly did not extend to times with his family.

They'd met. The words reverberated through her mind over and over again. A two-word refrain with the power to torture her emotions as effectively as a rack and bullwhip.

She did not know why he had slept with her that night in Marsala. She had no clue why he had taken her to his bed in his family home, but she knew why he hadn't called her for two weeks and had ignored her calls to him.

Perhaps he regretted that intimacy and was even hoping to end their association.

The pain that thought brought her doubled her over, and she had to pull to the side of the road. Tears came then.

She never cried, but right now she could not stop.

She sobbed, the sounds coming from her mouth like those of a wounded animal, and she had no way of stopping them, of pulling her cheerful covering around her and marching on with a smile on her face. Not now.

She had thought maybe it was her turn for happiness. Maybe this baby heralded a new time in her life, one where she did not lose everyone who she loved.

But she could see already that was not true.

She had lost Tino, or was on the verge of doing so.

Her body racked with sobs, she ached with a physical pain no one was there to assuage.

What if Tino's rejection was merely a harbinger of things to come?

What if she lost this baby, too? She could not stand it.

The first trimester was a risky one, even though her doctor had confirmed her pregnancy was viable and not ectopic. The prospect of miscarriage was a dark, scary shadow over her mind.

Falling apart at the seams like this could not be helping, but she didn't know if she had the strength to rein the tears in. How was she supposed to buck up under this new loss?

The pain did not diminish, but eventually the tears did and she was able to drive home.

She had not lied when she told Agata she felt the need to create, but the piece she did that night was not one she wanted to share with anyone. Especially not a woman as kind as Tino's mother.

Faith could not make herself destroy it, though.

Once again it embodied pain she had been unable to share with anyone else.

It was another pregnant figure, but this woman was starving, her skin stretched taut over bones etched in sharp relief in the clay. Her clothes were worn and clung to the tiny bump that indicated her pregnancy in hopeless poverty. Her hair whipped around her face, raindrops mixed with tears on the visage of a mother-to-be almost certain not to make it another month, much less carry her baby to term.

The figure reflected the emotional starvation that had plagued Faith for so long. She'd tried to feed it like a beggar would her empty belly in the streets. Teaching children art, sharing their lives. Her friendship with Agata. Her intimacy with Tino, but all of it was as precarious as the statue woman's hold on life.

Faith had no one to absolutely call her own and feared that somehow the baby she carried would be lost to her as well.

She could not let that happen.

Valentino called Faith the next day. He'd tried calling the night before several times, after Gio had gone to bed, but she had not answered. He'd hoped to see her, but she had been ignoring the phone.

It was the first time she had done so during their association. He had not liked it one bit and had resolved not to avoid her calls in the future.

This time however, she answered on the third ring, just when he thought it was going to go to voice mail again.

"Hello, Tino."

"Carina."

"Do you need something?"

"No 'How was your trip?' or anything?"

"If you had wanted to tell me about your trip,

you would have called while you were away…
or answered my calls to you."

Ouch. "I apologize for not doing so. I was busy."
Which was the truth, just not the whole truth.

"Too busy for a thirty-second hello? I don't
think so."

"I should have called," he admitted.

"It doesn't matter."

"If it offended you, it does." Of course it had
offended her.

He would not have cared with any of the other
bed partners he had had since Maura's death,
but this was Faith. And he cared.

"I guess you didn't have time for phone sex
and saw no reason to speak to me otherwise,"
she said in a loaded tone.

He had already apologized. What more did
she want? "Now you are being foolish." They
had never engaged in phone sex, though the
thought was somewhat intriguing.

"I seem to make a habit of that with you."

"Not that I have noticed."

"Really?" She sighed, the sound coming across
the phone line crystal clear. "You must be blind."

Something was going on here. Something bad. Perhaps he owed her more than a verbal apology for avoiding her as he had done. It was imperative they meet. "Can we get together tonight?"

"For sex only or dinner first?"

What the hell? "Is it your monthly?"

She was usually disconcertingly frank about that particular time of month and did not suffer from a big dose of PMS, but there was a first time for everything. Right?

She gasped. There was a few seconds of dead air between them. Then she said, "No, Tino. I can guarantee you it is not that time of month."

Rather than apologize for his error yet again, he said, "It sounds like we would benefit from talking, Faith. Let's meet for dinner."

"Where?"

He named a restaurant and she agreed without her usual enthusiastic approval.

"Would you rather go somewhere else?" he asked.

"No."

"All right, then. Montibello's it is."

* * *

She was early, waiting at the table when he arrived. She looked beautiful as usual, but gave a dim facsimile of her normal smile of welcome.

He leaned down and kissed her cheek. "Did you have a good day?"

Looking away, she shrugged.

This was so not like her he really began to worry. Was she ill? Or returning to the States? His stomach plummeted at the thought. "Anything you want to talk about?"

"Not particularly."

Right. He was not buying that, but obviously she was hesitant. Maybe they could ease into whatever was making her behave so strangely by talking about other things. "There is something I think we should discuss."

"Fine." The word came out clipped and infused with attitude.

Okay, then. Reverse was not a gear he used often in his professional or personal life, so he went forward with the original plan. "We need to come up with a strategy for how we behave around my family."

"You really think that's going to become a

problem?" she asked in a mocking tone he'd never heard from her. "We've been sleeping together for months and have only been around them together twice in all that time. The first instance would not have occurred if you had known I was your son's teacher, and the second could have been avoided if I had known you were due to return a day earlier than expected."

"Nevertheless, the occasions did happen and I feel we should develop a strategy for dealing with similar ones when they happen again."

"I think you handled it already, Tino. Your family is under the impression we are something between bare acquaintances and casual friends." Her hands clenched tightly in her lap as she spoke.

He wanted to reach out and hold them, but that would be pushing the boundaries of what he considered safe public displays. Both for his sake and hers. He did not hide the fact that they saw each other, but he did not make it easy for others to guess at their relationship, either.

Marsala was a big enough city that he could take her to dinner at restaurants where he was unlikely to run into his business associates. Even less probable was the possibility of being seen by family. However, there were still some small-town ideals in Marsala, and Faith, as a single woman, could not afford to have her reputation tarnished if she wanted to continue teaching art at the elementary school.

"Did my saying that bother you?" Surely she understood the implications if he had reacted differently.

"Does it matter? Our relationship, such that it is, has never been about what I was comfortable with." Her eyes were filled with a hurt anger that shocked him.

"That is not true. You were no more interested in a long-term committed relationship than I was when we first met."

"Things change."

"Some things cannot." He wished that was not the case, but it was. "We do not have to lose what we do have because it cannot be *more*."

"You spent two weeks ignoring me, Tino."

"I was out of country."

It was a lame excuse and her expression said

she knew it. "You forwarded my calls to voice mail."

"I needed a breathing space. I had some things to work out," he admitted. "But I have apologized. I will do so again if that will improve things for you."

She flicked her hand as if dismissing his offer. "Did you work out your *problems?*"

"I believe so."

"And it included treating me like a nonentity in your life in front of your family?" she asked with a definite edge to her voice.

"If I had not, my mother would have gotten wind of our relationship. She knows me too well."

At that moment, Faith's eyes reflected pure sorrow. "And that would have been a catastrophe?"

"Yes." He hated giving the confirmation when she looked so unhappy about the truth, but he had no choice. "It would not be appropriate to have my mistress visiting with my family."

"I am not your mistress."

"True, but were I to try to explain the distinction to Mama, she would have us married faster than the speed of light. She likes you, Faith, and she wants more grandchildren from her oldest son."

"And the thought of marriage to me is a complete anathema to you?"

No, it was not, but that was a large part of the problem. "I do not wish to marry anyone."

"But you would do so."

"If I was absolutely convinced that was what was best for Giosue." Only, he would not marry a woman he could love, a woman who could undermine his honor.

Faith nodded and stood.

"Where are you going? We have not even ordered."

"I'm not hungry, Tino."

He stood as well. "Then we will leave."

"No."

"What do you mean?" Panic made his words come out hard and clipped.

"It's over. I don't want to see you anymore." Tears washed into her peacock-blue eyes.

For a moment they sparkled like grieving sapphires, but she blinked the moisture away along with any semblance of emotion from her face.

He could not believe the words coming out of her mouth, much less the way she seemed to be able to turn off her feelings. It was as if a stranger, not the woman he had been making love to for almost a year, stood across from him. "Because I needed some space and neglected to call you for two weeks?"

"No, though honestly? That would be enough for most women."

"You are not most women."

"No, I've been a very convenient sexual outlet, but that's over, Tino. The well is dried up." A slight hitch in her voice was the only indication she felt anything at all at saying these words.

"What the blazes are you talking about?" The well? What bloody well?

She talked like he'd been using her this past year, but there relationship had been mutual.

"You wanted me just as I wanted you."

She shrugged. *Shrugged,* damn it. Just as if this conversation wasn't of utmost importance.

"Along with agreeing that this thing between us wasn't some serious emotional connection, we also agreed that if it stopped working for either of us, we were completely free to walk away. No harm. No foul. I'm walking." Her voice was even and calm, free of her usual passion and any feeling—either positive or negative.

"How can you go from wanting more to wanting nothing?" he asked, dazed by this turn of events.

"You aren't going to give me more, and nothing is a better option than settling for what we had."

"There was no settling. You wanted me as much as I wanted you," he said again, as if repeating it might make her get the concept.

"Things change."

He cursed loudly, using a word in the Sicilian vernacular rarely heard in polite company.

"You promised."

"What did I promise?"

"To let me walk away without a big scene."

Damn it all to hell. He had, but he had never expected her to want to walk away. "What about my mother?"

"What about her? She's my friend."

"And my son?"

"He is my student."

"You do not intend to ditch either of them?"

"No."

"Only me."

"It's necessary."

"For who?"

"For me."

"Why?"

"What difference does it make? You won't give me more and I can't accept less any longer. The whys don't matter."

"I don't believe that."

"Not my problem."

"I did not know you had this hard side to you."

"I wasn't aware you could be so clingy."

Affronted at the very implication, he ground out, "I am *not* clingy."

"I'm glad to hear it. Goodbye, Tino. I'm sure I'll be seeing you around."

"Wait, Faith…"

But she was gone and the maître d' was apologizing and offering to move their table, asking what they had done to offend. Valentino had no answers for the man. He had no answers for himself.

In a near catatonic state of shock, Faith stood beside her car outside the restaurant. The coldness she had felt toward Tino at the table had permeated her body until she felt incapable of movement.

She had broken up with him.

Really, truly. Not a joke. Not with tears, or hopes he would try to talk her out of it, but with a gut-deep certainty the relationship they had, such as it was, was over.

She hadn't gone to the restaurant with the intention of breaking up. Had she?

She knew her pregnancy hormones had her emotions on a see-saw and she'd been trying to ride them out. She laughed soundlessly, her heart aching. A see-saw? More like an emotional roller coaster of death-defying height, speed and terrifying twists and turns.

She didn't just teeter from one feeling to the next, she swooped without warning.

It hadn't been easy the two weeks he had avoided her calls, but it had been even worse since Tino had denied their friendship to his mother. Faith had realized that what she believed was affection had only been the result of lust on his part. He wanted sex and she gave it to him. Only, she couldn't do that anymore.

She wouldn't risk the baby.

The doctor had said normal sexual activity wouldn't jeopardize her pregnancy, but then he didn't know her past, how easily she lost the people who meant the most to her. She'd known she would have to put Tino off from being physically intimate for at least another few weeks, but she hadn't realized that somewhere deep inside that had meant breaking things off with him completely.

It had all crystallized when he said he wouldn't marry her—at any cost. Once he knew about the baby, that attitude would change, but the underlying reasons for it wouldn't. She knew that. Just as she knew that a marriage made for reasons of duty and responsibility was the last kind she wanted.

It was one thing to marry someone knowing you loved them and they only liked you and found deep satisfaction in your body. But to marry someone you knew did *not* want to marry you and did in fact see something so wrong about you that they would marry someone else over you, that was something else entirely.

She wasn't sure she could do it.

But could she take the baby from Sicily, from its family and raise it alone, knowing it could have a better life in its father's home country? She didn't know. Thankfully, that decision did not have to be made right this second.

She forced her frozen limbs to move, and slid into her car, turning on the ignition.

She drove toward her home while those questions and more plagued her. Plagued by a question she told herself did not need an immediate answer. Her mind refused to let it go, the only eye in the storm of her emotion being that she had no intention of revealing her pregnancy until she was through the more-dangerous first trimester.

At that point she would have to have answers.

* * *

Though she normally saw the older woman at least once a week, Faith managed to avoid showing Agata the pregnancy statuary. Faith promised Tino's mother she would be the first to see all the pieces for the new show she was putting together for a New York gallery. Faith had sent pictures of the pieces she'd been doing to a gallery owner on Park Avenue who loved TK's work. The woman had called Faith, practically swooning with delight at the prospect of doing a show for the fertility pieces.

Like her emotions, Faith's work swung between hope and despair, touching on every emotion in between. It was the most powerful stuff she'd done since the car accident that had stolen her little family. As much pain as some of the pieces caused her, she was proud of them all.

An art teacher had once told Faith's class that pain was a great source of inspiration, as was joy, but that either without the other left an artist's work lacking in some way. Faith was living proof both agony and ecstasy could reside side by side in a person's heart. And she had no doubt her work was all the better for it, even if her heart wasn't.

Tino tried calling Faith several times, but his calls were sent straight to voice mail every time. He left messages but they were ignored. He sent her text messages that received no reply either.

He could not believe his affair with Faith was over.

He wouldn't believe it.

She wasn't acting like herself, and he was going to find out why. And fix it, damn it.

Morning sickness was just that for Faith, with the nausea dissipating by noon. While that did not impact her ability to work much, it did make it more difficult on the days she taught. She'd considered canceling her classes for the first trimester, or withdrawing all together. She doubted they would want an unwed pregnant woman teaching art to their children; it was a traditional village. However, she saw little Gio only on the days she taught and she could not make herself give up those visits, brief though they were.

She loved the little boy. A lot. She hadn't realized how much she had come to see him as something more than a pupil, something like family—until she broke things off with his father and contemplated not seeing the precious boy again. She simply could not do it.

He was as sweet as ever, showing he had no idea she was now persona non grata in his papa's life. He hung back after class to talk to her and she enjoyed that. Today, though, he was fidgeting.

"Is something the matter, sweetheart?"

He grinned. "I like it when you call me that. It's like a mama would do, you know?"

Suppressing the stab of pain at his words, she reached out and brushed his hair back from his face. "I'm glad. Now, tell me if something is wrong."

"Nonna said I could invite you for dinner."

"That is very kind of her."

"Only, Papa said you probably wouldn't come."

"He did?"

Gio looked at her with pleading eyes only a heart of stone could ignore. "Why won't you come again? I thought you and Papa were friends."

"I didn't say I wouldn't come."

"So, you will?" Giosue asked, his little-boy face transforming with the light of hope.

"When does your *nonna* want me to come?"

"She said this Friday would be good."

"It just so happens I am free this Friday."

Gio grinned with delight and gave her a spontaneous hug that went straight to her heart.

Perhaps it was foolish to agree, but she couldn't stand to see the hurt of disappointment come into Giosue's eyes. Besides, Faith had told Tino that she had no intention of giving up her friendship with his mother and son. And she'd meant it.

Being pregnant with Giosue's sibling and Agata's grandchild only made those two relationships more important. Tino wasn't going away and she needed to work on her ability to be around him and remain unaffected. The dinner invitation was an opportunity to do just that.

Her unborn baby deserved to know his or her family and Faith would not allow her own feelings to stand in the way of that.

Besides there was a tiny part of her that wanted to show Tino he was wrong and that she could handle being around him just fine.

Just a small part. Really.

CHAPTER SEVEN

LESS CERTAIN OF HER ABILITY to withstand Tino's company unscathed than she had been in the safety of her art classroom, Faith rang the doorbell of the big villa.

The door opened almost immediately, making her heart skip a beat. However, it was only Giosue on the other side.

Relief flooded her, making her smile genuine. "Good evening, Gio."

"Bueno sera, signora."

She handed him a small gift.

"What is this?" he asked, his voice tinged with anticipation mixed with confusion.

"It is traditional to give one's dinner host a gift. I forgot yours when you invited me before, so I've brought it tonight along with one for your grandmother."

"Because this time she invited you?"

"Exactly."

Gio looked at the present and then up at her, his eyes shining. "Wow. Can I open it now?"

She nodded.

He ripped the package apart with the enthusiasm usually reserved for the young and sucked in a breath as he saw what was inside. They were leather gardening gloves made to fit a child's hands.

"I didn't know if you already had a pair…"

"I do, but they are made of cloth and not nearly so nice. Come, I want to show Nonno."

She smiled, glad her gift had gone over so well, and followed Gio to the lanai, Agata's favorite place to entertain. When they arrived, she saw both Agata and Rocco, but no Tino.

Relieved at what she was sure would be only a temporary respite, Faith watched Gio run to his grandfather to show him the new gloves.

Agata smiled in welcome and hugged Faith, kissing both her cheeks. "It is good to see you."

"Come, Mama, you speak as if it had been weeks rather than a few days since the last time you saw your friend." There was an edge to Tino's voice that Faith could not miss.

She wondered if Agata noticed, but the older woman seemed to be oblivious.

Shaking her head at her son, who had just arrived, she said, "Faith is a dear friend I would see every day if I could. She is good for Gio too."

"Save your matchmaking attempts for someone susceptible, Mama. I do not believe Faith likes me at all."

Oh, he was in fine form tonight. Faith refused to rise to the bait and show her chagrin at his words.

"Nonsense. You're my son, what is not to like?" Agata demanded.

Faith could make a list, but she forebore doing so for Agata's sake. See? She could handle this. She *would* handle this.

Her desire to strangle Tino for his leading comment morphed to unwilling concern as she saw how haggard he looked. Oh, he was his usual gorgeous self, but there was a certain cast to his skin and lines around his eyes that were not usually there—all of it bespeaking a bone-deep exhaustion.

"You look tired," she blurted out.

"*Si,* this one has been working too many hours. Like a man possessed, he returns to his office after our little Gio goes to sleep and works into the early hours before returning home."

"I told you, I have some things going on that require extra attention right now."

Agata frowned. "You say that to your father and maybe he will believe you. Men! But I am your mother and you are behaving much the same as you did after Maura's death. I do not understand it."

"There is nothing to understand. I am not grieving, I am working." He said it with so much force, Faith couldn't help believing.

Agata did not look so convinced. But then, she was a mother and tended to see the softer side of her child, even if such a side did not exist.

"Is the new venture going well?"

"Yes." Tino's voice was clipped and the look he threw his mother was filled with frustration.

"Regardless of what my family thinks, I am damn good at my job."

Rocco had joined them and was shaking his head. "Of course we know you are a success. How could you be anything else? You are my son, no? And I am the greatest vintner in Sicily. Why should you not be a businessman of equal talent? You are a Grisafi."

Faith was tempted to laugh, but knew Rocco would not take it well. He was serious. Of course. But Faith had no problem seeing where Tino got his arrogance from.

"He is that," Agata said with asperity. "Which means that in this home, he is my son, not some bigshot businessman. And you are my husband, not the maker of the best wines in the country."

"Yes, of course." Rocco did not look the least cowed, but sounded more than willing to be compliant.

Agata shook her head. "Men!"

It was a word she said often over the next few hours, with the same slightly exasperated and amused tone. Faith was gratified that despite the stress of being around Tino, she found the evening highly entertaining and surprisingly comfortable.

So long as she avoided direct contact with her former lover, that is. It wasn't easy in such a small group.

And Tino wasn't helping. He had to know she found being around him difficult, but he engaged her in conversation, and she barely avoided sitting beside him at dinner. In that, Gio was her unwitting accomplice.

However, once dinner had been eaten, it was clear that Gio and Agata both intended to see that Faith and Tino spend as much time together as possible.

Right now she was being given a tour of the vineyard, ostensibly by Rocco. Only, the old man and Gio often moved ahead, or lingered behind, leaving her alone with Tino for brief spurts of time.

"You never answered my mother's question," Tino said during one of those moments.

"I don't know what you mean."

"She asked what there was about me not to like."

"She's biased. She's your mother."

"*Si,* but that's not the point."

"And what is the point?"

"That you never answered her question."

"She didn't seem bothered by that." The older woman had not brought it up again.

"Perhaps not, but I am."

"That's too bad. I'm not here to visit with you, Tino."

"My family will be disappointed. They are matchmaking."

"In vain."

"Yes, but won't you tell me why?"

He was insane. He was the one who refused to consider marriage. Ultimately, wasn't that a far more effective deterrent to his family's attempts at matchmaking than her supposed dislike of him?

"You're arrogant."

"I am a Grisafi."

"So, it comes with the territory?"

"Definitely."

She rolled her eyes.

"What else?"

"I never said I didn't like you, Tino." And

she couldn't do so now in honesty. He'd hurt her, but she did like him. She loved the callous lout, but yes, she liked him, too. Just not some of his attitudes.

"You said you never wanted to see me again."

"I said our affair was over."

"And yet here you are."

"Visiting your family, Tino. Not you!"

"You could have arranged to come a different night."

"Why should I?"

He laughed, the sound too sexy for her peace of mind. And highly annoying. "Ah, proving me wrong, Faith? Making sure that I know I don't matter enough for you to avoid dinner in my home?"

"I told you I wouldn't give up my friendship with your mother or son."

"You wanted to see me, or you would not have come tonight." He brushed her cheek with his hand. "Admit it."

She jumped back from the gentle touch that felt like a brand. "If I hadn't come, your parents would have suspected something was wrong between us. I would think *you* would have realized that and tried to avoid it. You could have made arrangements to be gone tonight without causing suspicion."

"I had no desire to do so." He shrugged, looking scarily determined.

"I don't see why."

"You have refused to answer my calls for the past week."

"That should have given you a message."

"It did. Something is wrong and I want to know what."

"I told you."

"You want more or nothing at all."

"Yes."

"I cannot give you marriage, Faith."

"You would be surprised at what you are capable of giving in the right circumstances, Tino." Why she said it, she didn't know.

The need to challenge him?

"What circumstances would those be?"

She shook her head, absolutely not going there right now. "Just leave it alone."

"I cannot."

"You have to."

"I know about your lost husband and child. I am sorry. If I could take that old pain away, I would. But I cannot fill the gap they left in your life. That is not in my power."

Did he really believe that? And here she'd thought he was smart. "You have your own past tragedies to deal with," was all she said.

He did not get a chance to answer because they caught up with Gio and Rocco. Faith was given a fascinating description of what happened to the grapes once they were picked. She found it difficult to focus on, however with Tino a brooding presence beside her.

They were once again on their own as Gio and his grandfather had hurried back to the house much too quickly for Faith to keep up in her high-heeled sandals. "How did you find out about Taylish and Kaden?" she asked, posing the question to Tino she could not get out of her mind.

"My mother."

Stunned, Faith stopped walking altogether. She could not imagine Agata sharing Faith's confidences without a prompting to do so. Not even in the effort to matchmake. "You asked her?"

"Yes." Tino stood only a couple of feet away, but the moonlight was not strong enough to illuminate the expression in his eyes.

She could feel its intensity though.

"Wasn't that dangerous?"

"In what way?"

She rolled her eyes, though she doubted he could see it. "Don't play dumb. It showed a more-than-passing interest in me."

Something he'd said he didn't want his mother to get wind of.

"It was worse than that, even," he said, sounding rueful, but not particularly bothered. "I allowed it to slip that we had discussed the statue in my bedroom."

Did he have any idea what he was revealing of his inner thoughts? Tino—Mr. Certainty, the man who never changed his mind and always knew best—was acting as if he did not know his own mind. Acting in direct opposition to his stated purpose. Maybe he had a deeper insight into the long-term effect of his words than she did.

She shook her head. "You're kidding."

"Sometimes my curiosity gets the better of me." He did not shrug, but the negligent movement was there in his voice.

"I guess," she said with emphasis. "I don't see your mother making a list of wedding guests as you feared."

"She is matchmaking, but being surprisingly low-key about it."

"And that doesn't bother you?"

"That she is matchmaking?"

"Yes." What the heck did he think she meant?

"So long as she maintains subtlety and does not make it into a family argument of dramatic proportions, no."

Maybe she understood his insouciance better now. "In other words, as long as it's easy for you to avoid the outcome she is looking for."

"You could put it that way."

"I just did."

"Si."

"Don't play with me, Tino."

He closed the distance between them but did not touch her. "I am not playing. I want you back."

"As your mistress."

"And my friend."

"That's not what you told your mother."

"I explained that."

"And I found your explanation lacking."

"Faith—"

Lucky for her, because she really didn't want to get into this right now—or ever really—Giosue came running up. "You two are too slow. Nonna said we could swim if you wanted, *signora*."

Faith moved toward Gio, putting distance between herself and his father once again. "Actually, I think it is time I returned home."

There was that look, the disappointment Faith hated to see, but Gio did not attempt to cajole her. He simply nodded and looked down at the ground.

And it was more effective than any type of whining might have been.

She grabbed his hand and said, "Maybe just a short swim. All right?"

He looked up at her, eyes shining. "Really, *signora?*"

"Yes."

"We can play water ball. *Zio* Calogero sent me a new net."

Faith had seen the basketball net attached to the side of the pool on a short pole. "That sounds like fun."

"Yes, it does." Tino took Gio's other hand. "Your papa will join you as well. Provided I am invited?"

"Of course, Papa." Gio's voice rang with joy.

And why shouldn't it? This was exactly what her favorite pupil wanted—the three of them together. Faith had wanted it, too, but she couldn't fight a ghost.

Tension filled her as she contemplated the next thirty minutes. She hadn't counted on Tino joining them in the pool, but she would have to deal with it. She wasn't about to renege on her promise to Gio. Though, for the first time in her life she was seriously tempted to back out on a commitment she'd made to a child.

Fifteen minutes later she was desperate enough to do so.

Tino had been teasing her, touching her under the guise of the game. A caress down her arm. A hand cupped over her hip. An arm around her waist, ostensibly to stop her from going under. But the final straw was when he brushed his lips over the sensitive spot behind her ear and whispered that he wanted her.

She shoved herself away from him and climbed out of the pool in the space of a couple seconds.

"*Signora,* where are you going?"

"It is time for me to leave." She tried to keep the frustration and anger she felt from her voice. It was not Gio's fault his father was a fiend.

"But why?" The little boy's eyes widened with confusion. "We were having fun."

"*Si.* I thought we were having a great deal of fun," Tino said with a purr.

"Really?" she asked—this time making no effort to hide her displeasure. "I'll leave it to you to explain to your son why I need to leave, then."

It was Tino's turn to look confused and he was the mirror image of his son in that moment, only older. Would their child take after him or her? What was she thinking about? This was not the time to consider whether the baby in her womb would resemble its father. Not when she wanted to bean the man.

Without another word, she spun on her heel and stormed to the cabana where she changed back into her clothes. A shower would have to wait until she got home.

She left moments later after hugging Agata and a hastily dried Gio. Rocco had gone to check on something in the wine cellars.

Her goodbye to Tino was perfunctory and verbal only.

Valentino stood outside Faith's apartment in Pizzolato, uncharacteristically hesitant to knock. The evening before had been an exercise in frustration for him. Every time he got a step closer to Faith, she took two backward. And he did not understand why.

He'd used their time in the pool to remind her of what they were both missing. Valentino was sure it had been working, too. Faith's breath had shortened, her nipples growing hard under her one-piece swimsuit. Heaven above knew he'd been hard enough to drill through cement.

But then she had pushed away from him with the clear intent to reject and climbed from the pool, saying she had to go. She didn't back down, either, not even when Gio looked heart-broken.

She'd left him there to explain her precipitous departure to his upset son.

What the hell was going on with her?

It was not like her to be so unfeeling. But the look she'd given him could have stripped paint.

It had been weeks since they made love in his family home, but it was not merely her body he craved. He missed her. Like an ache in his gut that no medication could take away. Which was why he was here right now, ready to make it right.

Whatever *it* was.

He gave the closed door a glare. What was he? A wimp? He did not think so. Not Valentino Grisafi.

He knocked on the door. Loudly.

His mother had told him that Faith got caught up in her work and didn't hear the door lots of times. That she worked whenever the mood struck her, the hour of the day not a deterrent no matter how late or early. She'd said a lot more about Faith.

Add this knowledge to everything she'd told him previously about TK, and Valentino had a completely new picture of his lover, an image that convicted him about how little he'd known before. Not that it should have mattered, but with Faith it did. Their relationship would be a year old in two more weeks, and he didn't want to spend the anniversary of their first date grieving her loss.

Taking a deep breath, he knocked again.

"Coming," came from inside.

A few seconds later the door swung open. "Agata, I wasn't expect—"

"My mother is at a fundraising meeting for Giosue's school, I believe."

Faith looked at him with something like resignation and sighed. "Yes. That's what I thought she was doing."

"Are you going to invite me in?"

"Will you go away if I don't?"

"No."

"Why do you want to come in? You've never

stepped foot in my building, much less my apartment. I didn't think you even knew where I lived."

He hadn't. He'd had to ask his mother, but Faith didn't need to know that. "I want to see where you work."

She grimaced, but stepped back. He followed her into the apartment. It wasn't huge, but it wasn't small, either. She'd converted the main living area, which opened to a glassed-in balcony, into her studio. The half-glass ceiling bathed the room in the glow of natural light, and he could easily see why she'd picked this location to work.

Although the area was clearly a working studio, she had created a conversation area in one corner with a love seat and two chairs around a low table decorated with traditional Sicilian tiles.

He settled into one of the chairs after declining a drink. "Is my mother the only person who visits you here?"

"No, a couple of the teachers from the school have been by, as well, but since the school day is not yet over..." She let her explanation trail off.

"What about other artists?" He was trying to

get a picture of her life, but it was still pretty fuzzy and that bothered him.

She gave a half shrug. "I'm a private person."

"You always came off as friendly and outgoing to me."

She wiped at a spot of clay on her hand with the rag she held as she took the seat farthest from his. "Yes, well, maybe I should say that TK is a private person. I have some friends in the artistic community, but none of them live close enough to drop in during the middle of the day."

He considered this and what she had said about other teachers coming over sometimes, which he read to mean rarely. "You're a very solitary person, aren't you?"

She shook her head, not in negation, but as if she couldn't think what to say. "Why are you here, Tino?"

After last night she could ask that?

"I miss you." There. The bald-faced truth.

"I don't see why you should." She stiffened, drawing herself up into a ramrod sitting posture. "You still have your hand."

Shock struck him like a bolt of lightning,

making it hard to breathe for just a second. "That is crude, and implies our relationship is nothing but mechanical sex."

"We no longer have a relationship."

He did not accept that, but to say so would violate their initial agreement. He decided to change the subject instead.

"Are those the pieces my mother is salivating to see?" he asked, referring to several cloth-covered shapes around the room.

"Yes. I told her she could see them when they are finished."

Sharp curiosity filled him. "She likes to see your work in progress." *He* wanted to see Faith's work.

"Not this time."

"Why not?"

"I don't want her to see them before they are cast and glazed."

"You are using the clay as models?"

"For some. There will be a numbered series cast before I break the mold for several, but some will be fired as is and be one-of-a-kind pieces."

"I know very little about your process." Even less than he knew about her.

"True." She didn't look inclined to elaborate.

But didn't most people enjoy rhapsodizing about their passions? From the way her work took over her home, he assumed her art was Faith's biggest passion. "Perhaps you would care to change that now?"

"I don't think so."

Her negative response stunned him. Though why it should, in the face of the way she'd been behaving, he didn't know. He kept expecting her to go back to acting the way she had until a few short weeks ago. "You don't feel like talking about your work?"

"I don't feel like talking to you."

"Don't be like that, *carina*." He didn't want to examine the way that made him feel, but it was not good. "We are friends."

"That's not what you told your mother."

Must she keep harping on that one moment in time, an answer to his mother's questioning he was past regretting and into mentally banging his head against a wall? "I was protecting myself, I admit it. But I was trying to protect us too, Faith. What would you have had me tell her?"

"The truth?"

"That we are lovers?" He did not think so.

She glared, her eyes snapping with anger and something akin to disgust. "That wouldn't be true, though, would it?"

"We are lovers, perhaps on hiatus, but still together."

"You are delusional. We are not and never were lovers."

"*Now* who is being delusional?"

She stood up, her hands fisted at her sides. "You have to give more than sex to be considered someone's lover. We were *sex partners*. Now we are past acquaintances."

"That is not true. We have more than sex between us." After all, that "more" had cost him the sleep of several nights.

"Oh, really?"

"Yes, *our friendship*."

"Again, let me refer you to that afternoon by the pool at your family home. You told your mother we were not friends."

"I made a mistake." There, he had said it. "I am sorry," he gritted.

"That was really hard for you, wasn't it?"

He just looked at her.

"Admitting you were wrong isn't your thing."

"It doesn't happen very often."

"Being wrong or admitting it?" she asked with dark amusement.

"Both."

"I don't suppose it does."

He too stood, taking her by the arms and standing close. "Let me back in, Faith. I need you." Those last three words were said even less frequently than an apology by him.

Tears filled her eyes. "I can't, Tino."

"Why not?"

She just shook her head.

"Tell me what is wrong. Let me make it right." He felt like he was drowning, but that wasn't right. He did not want this thing between them to end, but if it did, it shouldn't be *this* wrenching.

"You can't make it right."

"I can try."

"Can you love *me?* Can you make me your wife?"

Something inside him shattered. "No."

"Then you can't fix it."

CHAPTER EIGHT

FAITH spent the next few days in a borderline state where the numbness of loss fought the tendrils of hope each day her pregnancy continued. She missed Tino. She wanted him—both emotionally and physically. She craved his touch, but not in a sexual way, and he didn't want her to give him anything else. She wanted to be held, cuddled and comforted as her body went through the changes pregnancy brought. She wanted someone to talk to in the evenings when she found herself too tired to create but too restless to sleep.

She had not realized how much his presence in her life staved off the loneliness, until he was gone. She found herself in a pathetic state of anticipation every time she spoke to Agata, hoping the Sicilian woman would drop news about her oldest son.

Faith's morning sickness had gotten worse the past few days, but she was more adamant than ever she would not give up her job teaching. She'd lost Tino. She didn't think she could stand to lose her only contact with his son, as well. When had the little boy become so important to her? She didn't know, but she could not deny that the love she felt for the child growing inside her was in equal intensity for the emotion she felt toward her former lover's son.

One evening, almost a week after Tino had left her apartment, she got a phone call from Agata.

"*Ciao, bella.* How are you?"

"Fine."

"You were not home today."

"No, I went shopping in Marsala." She'd needed to get out. To be around other people. There were moments when she felt she was going mad from loneliness.

"I stopped by hoping to have lunch."

"Oh," Faith said with genuine regret. "I'm so sorry I missed you."

"Yes, well, I would only have begged you to show me your work."

Faith laughed. "Soon." She knew just how she was going to announce her pregnancy to her dear friend, but not until the risky first trimester was past.

How she was going to tell Agata that the baby was Tino's was less clear however.

"I would like that." There was an emotional note in Agata's tone that surprised Faith, but maybe it shouldn't have.

She'd never known another human being as connected to her art as the older woman. Not even Taylish had understood the emotion behind the pieces the way Agata did.

"So, how about lunch tomorrow?" Agata asked.

"That would be lovely."

They rang off and Faith turned to face her empty apartment, wondering if her newfound evening nausea would allow her to eat an evening meal.

Valentino's mother took the seat beside where he watched his son frolic in the pool with his papa.

The worried expression on her face concerned Valentino. He knew she had planned to call Faith. "Mama, what is the matter?"

His mother twisted her hands in an uncharacteristic display of nerves but did not answer.

"Mama."

She looked up as if just realizing he was sitting there. "Oh, did you say something, son?"

"I asked if there was anything the matter."

"Nothing bad. Well, there may well be ramifications, but I'm in a quandary and do not know what to do."

"About what?" he asked with some impatience. Was this about Faith?

His mother sighed heavily. "I did something I should not have."

"What?"

"I do not think I should say."

Valentino waited patiently. He knew his mother. She would not have said anything if she did not want to confess to someone. Apparently, he was that someone. And if it was related to Faith in any way, he was glad.

Not that he should be pining over the woman who dumped him like yesterday's garbage. She'd thrown down her ultimatum and he had

refused terms. She'd been unwilling to nego-
tiate—that should be the end of it.

Still, he waited with uncomfortable anticipation for his mother to speak.

She sighed again. Fidgeted some more and
then sighed a third time. "I have a key to Faith's
apartment."

"Ah." But he didn't feel nearly as insouciant
as he sounded. His mother had a key to his
lover's apartment, but he did not. Nor did Faith
have a key to his apartment in Marsala. Why
not? Why was it that his mother had spent more
time in Faith's studio than he had?

They were friends. They did not limit their time
together to sex. So, why had he never seen any
of her works in progress? Why had he not known
she was the highly successful sculptor TK?

"I stopped by today. Unannounced."

"I see." Though he didn't.

"I let myself in, you know, thinking she might
be back soon." Mama shuddered. "I did a
terrible thing."

"You are not the criminal type. I doubt what
you did was *terrible*."

"But it *was,* my son. I wanted so badly to see Faith's newest work."

"You peeked."

"Yes, and that is bad enough—but in looking at her work, I revealed a secret she is clearly not ready to share."

"A secret?" What kind of secret? Had Faith been making clay tiles of the fifty states because she missed her homeland? What?

"*Si.* A secret. I have betrayed my friend."

"Mama, whatever it is, I am sure it will be fine. Faith loves you. She will forgive you." If only Faith was as tolerant of her lover.

"But a woman has the right to determine the timing of when she will share such news with others. I have, what is that saying your brother uses—oh, yes—I have stolen her thunder. I cannot pretend not to know when she tells me, for that would be a lie. I cannot lie to my friend." She grimaced. "I did tell her I still wanted to see her work and I do. I stopped looking after the first one because I knew. I knew what it meant."

Valentino ground his teeth and tried not to

glare at his mother with impatience. "What *what* meant?"

"The statue. It is so clear to see. You could not miss it," she said, as if trying to convince Valentino.

"I am sure you are right. What was the statue of?" he asked without being able to help himself.

"It is just that I am so worried. If it means what I think, and I'm sure it does—and there is no father in sight. Things are going to get difficult for my friend."

"What does a priest have to do with Faith?"

"A priest? Who said anything about a priest? Faith is Lutheran. They have pastors, I believe."

"Mama, I don't understand. You said 'father.'"

"Yes, the father of her child."

"Child? Faith has no children. Her unborn baby died in the accident with her husband."

"The baby inside her now, Valentino."

Valentino's chest grew tight. Although he knew he was breathing, it felt like all the oxygen had disappeared from the air. "Are you saying you believe Faith is pregnant?"

"Of course that is what I have been saying. Weren't you listening? I should never have snooped. Now when she tells me, I will have to admit I already guessed. She will be let down."

His mother continued to talk, but Valentino did not hear what she said. He had surged to his feet and was trying to rush across the brickwork of the patio. But his movements were uncoordinated and jerky as his mother's words reverberated inside his head like clanging cymbals in a discordant rhythm.

Faith was pregnant?

His Faith? The woman who said she did not want to see him anymore. The one who had ended their relationship, such as it was.

He shook his head, but the blanket of shock refused to be dislodged.

He was going to be a father again? Now? When he had thought never to remarry, when he had believed Giosue would be his only child. It was unreal but not. Part of him accepted the news with an atavistic instinct of rightness. He had no doubt the baby was his. Dismiss him though she had tried to do, Faith was his. She had been since the moment they met. Hell, a primal part of him claimed she always had been—even before they knew each other.

Even the most rational part of his mind accepted that she was his *now*. She had been with no one else since their first time together, and probably for a long time before that.

He yanked open the door of his Jaguar and climbed inside, slamming it again as he started the car with a loud roar of the engine, and then tearing out of the drive.

How was she pregnant?

They used birth control. Religiously. Rather, he did. Still, there had only been a handful of times that their protection had not been one hundred percent. After each slip, he would be beset by guilt, and work extrahard in future to make sure they were covered.

With a sense of inevitability, he realized one of those times had not been too long ago.

He'd taken Faith to dinner at a favorite trattoria. Instead of sitting outside, so they could watch people on the street—as Faith was wont to do—Valentino had asked for some privacy.

They had been given a table in the back corner, the restaurant lighting barely reaching into the shadows that surrounded it. The light from the single candle in the center of the table set a romantic mood.

At least, he'd thought so.

Faith frowned as he helped her take her seat. "I know our relationship isn't common knowledge, but do we have to hide in the dark?"

He leaned down and whispered in her ear. "I thought we could entertain ourselves over dinner, rather than finding our amusement in watching other people."

The embarrassing truth was that Faith liked people-watching—sometimes too much. She paid more attention to the ones surrounding them than to him, and he did not like that. Tonight he was determined to have her entire focus. If it took seducing her publicly, so be it.

And that is exactly what he did, starting with a kiss just below the shell of her ear, using both teeth and tongue as well as his lips.

She was shivering and had made a small whimpering sound by the time he finished and took his own seat across the small table from her.

"Considering what you apparently have planned for our *entertainment,* I now understand why you asked for a table hidden away from curious eyes." Faith smoothed her top, accentuating the way the silky fabric clung to her breasts and exposing hardened nipples, despite two thin layers of fabric over them.

"You think you can survive one evening without people-watching?" he asked, his voice husky with the desire sparking his senses.

"I have a feeling you can make it worth my while."

"You must be psychic," he teased. "For I plan to."

"Call it an educated guess. I've been at the receiving end of your tender mercies too often to discount their effect."

"Good." He had every intention of lavishing those mercies on her tonight.

They teased each other over dinner, working their desire to a fever pitch. He was tempted to find an even darker corner and bring them both to completion right then and there. He refrained, determined to make the night a memorable one for his beautiful lover.

Her peacock-blue eyes were glazed with passion, her lips swollen as if they'd been kissed, and her breathing was shallow and quick. Her nipples were so hard they created shoals in the fabric over them and she'd squirmed in her seat more than once.

"Having trouble, *carina americana mia?*" He meant his voice to be joking, but it came out deep and sensual instead.

A competitive glint shone in her gaze along with the passion. "I think no more than you."

She'd definitely done her utmost to turn him inside out, and she had succeeded.

He reached across the table and brushed her cheek in a rare public display of affection. "I think it is time to make our way to my apartment."

"*Yes.*"

Back in his apartment, they wasted no time in disposing of their clothing, but once they landed naked on the bed, he forced a slowing of the pace. It wasn't easy, he wanted nothing more than to bury himself in her wet, silken depths, but there was more to making love than reaching an orgasm.

There was the element of driving your partner out of her mind.

Her hands were everywhere in a blatant bid to sidetrack him from his silently stated intention, and he had to gather both her wrists in one hand and hold them above her head.

She gasped, her body bowing in clear need. "Kinky, Tino."

"Necessary, *tesoro*."

"Why?"

"I want you out of your mind with pleasure."

"I'm already there."

"No." He kissed her, sweeping her mouth with his tongue. He pulled back. "You can still talk."

And then he set about taking care of that. He kissed his way down her throat, sucking up a bruise in the dip right below her clavicle bone. His mark.

She shuddered and cried out, like she always did when his hormones got the best of him and he gave her a hickey like he was still an adolescent learning his way around a woman. Maybe that's why he regressed so often.

He moved to her breasts, taking one in his free hand and laving the other with his tongue. Eventually, after a lot of mewling and half-formed words from the dead-to-rights sexy woman below him, he zeroed in on her nipples. He didn't play. He focused. He plucked. And he pleasured.

She screamed.

She arched.

She came, her body going rigid and then shaking.

He released her hands and rolled on top of her, using the head of his penis to tease the swollen nub of her clitoris. She cried out incoherently and he kept it up. Her legs locked around his and she pressed upward, forcing him inside. He rocked and kissed her until he was on the verge of climaxing himself.

It was only then that he remembered the condom he wasn't wearing.

With more self-control than he thought he had, he pulled out and reached for the bedside drawer where he kept his supplies before surging back inside her.

When he came, she was screaming his name and convulsing around him in a second more-intense orgasm.

Remembering made him harder than a rock and twice as immovable.

That night had happened somewhere between two and three months ago. If he looked at his PDA, he could get an exact date. It was something he'd kept track of as zealously as he had their birth control itself. Only, the timing had never come to anything before. Maybe that was why he hadn't been worried along these lines in this instance?

The possibility that Faith might be carrying his child had not even occurred to him. Why would it? A woman didn't break up with the man whose child she carried.

He spit forth a vicious curse as he yanked the door open on his Jaguar. It was entirely too possible, though.

And rather than tell him, Faith had booted Valentino from her life.

Why? What was she thinking? Did she believe he would allow her to take his child back to America and raise it, ignorant of its Sicilian family?

Did she think he would not find out? That he would disappear from her life as easily as she dismissed him from hers?

She did not know him very well, if that was the case. It seemed they both had a great deal to learn about each other.

Something didn't make any sense, though. If she had wanted to marry him as she had hinted, why had she kept this a secret? Surely she knew he would never deny his child the right to his name and heritage. What was the matter with her?

Then he remembered how irrational Maura had gotten on a few occasions while she was pregnant with Giosue.

Faith was no doubt suffering the same emotional fragility. He would have to get himself under control. He could not allow the fury coursing through him a vent. Not in her current condition. He would have to remain calm.

And he would have to remember she was not thinking clearly.

It was his responsibility to make things right and that was something he was good at. Fixing things for others. Had he not taken a slowly sinking vineyard, at risk of closing its doors before the next generation was old enough to take over, and made it a diversified, multinational company?

He had saved the Grisafi heritage and when his younger brother and their father were at loggerheads, Valentino had salvaged the relationship by sending his brother across the ocean to run their offices in New York. The two strong-headed men spoke on the phone weekly and rarely argued any longer.

The only thing he had failed to fix was his wife's illness. He had not been able to save Maura, and he had paid the price for his inability, but he wasn't going to lose another woman who depended on him.

Loud knocking startled Faith from a fitful doze. She sat up, looking around her small apartment in disoriented semiwakefulness.

The pounding sounded again and she realized it was coming from her door. She stumbled to her feet and made her way toward it, swinging the door open just as Tino raised his hand to knock again.

He dropped his arm immediately, a look of relief disparate to the situation crossing his handsome features. "Thank the *madre vergine.* I tried knocking quietly, but you did not hear me." He reached out as if to touch her, but didn't—letting his hand drop to his side once again. "Were you working? Is that safe now? Do the clay or glazes have dangerous fumes? This is something we need to look into. I do not wish to demand you give up your passion, but it may be necessary for these final months."

"Tino?" Was she still too groggy to make sense of his words, or had her former lover lost his mind?

"*Si?*"

"You're babbling." She'd never heard him say so many words without taking a breath. And none of them made any sense. "You sound like your mother when she gets a bee in her bonnet."

"Mama does not keep insects in her wardrobe and she would not thank you for implying otherwise."

"It's an expression, for Heaven's sake. What is the matter with you tonight?"

"You need to ask me this?" he demanded in a highly censorious voice. His eyes closed and he groaned, just a little, but it was definitely a groan. "Excuse me, Faith."

"Uh, okay?" she asked, rather than said.

He took three deep breaths, letting each one out slower than the one before. Then he opened his eyes and looked at her with this Zen-like expression that was almost as weird as his babbling. "May I come in?"

"You're asking me?" Not demanding she invite him in. Not just forging ahead, assuming he was welcome? "What's going on, Tino?"

He didn't answer, simply giving the room behind her a significant look.

"Oh, all right. Come in." She stepped back.

It wasn't the most gracious invitation she had ever extended, but she was still disoriented from falling asleep after speaking to Agata on the phone. And Tino was acting strange.

Really. Really.

"Can I get you something to drink?"

"I could use a whiskey," he said in an odd tone. "But I will get it. You sit down."

"You've only been here once before, Tino. You don't know where I keep anything."

His hands fisted at his sides, but then the Zen thing was back and he said in a very patient tone, "So tell me."

She knew he wanted her back, but enough to sublimate his usually passionate nature? She would never have guessed.

"Why don't I just get us our drinks instead?"

"You aren't having whiskey, are you?"

She rolled her eyes. "I never drink hard spirits. You know that."

But he'd never acted as if he thought she shouldn't before. Though, considering how tipsy she got on a single glass of wine, perhaps his concern made a certain kind of sense. And honestly, she'd never implied she wanted to drink hard liquor before. But still. "What's the matter with you tonight?"

"We have things to discuss."

"We've done all the talking that needs doing." For right now, anyway. She was frankly too tired and too nauseous to rehash their breakup. She was feeling week and wishing he would just hold her.

She had to get a handle on these cravings. Or she was going to do something stupid, like ask him to fulfill them.

He didn't bother answering. He simply guided her back to the small love seat she'd been dozing on and pressed her to sit down. Bemused by his insistence on getting their beverages, she did. He then picked up her feet and turned her so that they rested on the love seat as well.

Apparently not content with that level of coddling, he tucked the throw she'd been sleeping under around her legs.

He nodded, as if in approval. "I will get our drinks now."

He was seriously working on getting back in her good graces. But no amount of tender care could make up for his refusal to see her as nothing more than a casual lover. Why couldn't he see that?

"If you insist on serving, I'd like a cup of tea." Something that hopefully would settle her tummy. "There is some ginger tea in the cupboard above the kettle. That's where you'll find the whiskey, as well."

An unopened bottle she had purchased in the hope that one day he would break his pattern and show enough interest in her life outside their sexual trysts to come see her.

He went to the kitchen area, nothing more than an alcove off the main living area, really. She watched him fill the kettle and flip the switch to heat the water. The domesticity of the scene tugged at her helter-skelter emotions. It was so much like something she wanted to experience all the time—for the right reasons— that stupid tears burned her eyes before she resolutely blinked them away.

He pulled down the box of tea and the bottle of whiskey from the cupboard. "I've never had ginger tea before."

She had. When she'd been pregnant before. And she was one of the lucky women it helped. "It's not something I drink often."

He gave her an enigmatic look but said nothing as he poured his own drink and waited for her water to boil.

She didn't ask him why he was there or what he wanted to talk about, because the answer was obvious. He wanted her back in his bed, but she'd do her best to avoid that particular conversation. "How is Gio?"

"You saw him only three days ago."

She shrugged. "I wish I taught more days a week," she admitted, before her brain caught up with her mouth.

"I understand."

"You do?"

"You hold my son in deep affection."

"He's easy to love."

"I agree."

"Um…"

"He wishes he could see you more often, as well."

"I know." Only, his father did not want them to grow closer. He'd made that clear.

"I think we can rectify that problem soon enough."

How? Was he going to up the ante of getting her back in bed by offering time with his family on a regular basis? Her rather creative and active imagination offered up a second option. One a lot less palatable.

Maybe he had decided to remarry after all. To find the paragon of Sicilian virtue he thought Gio deserved as a stepmother. Someone who would eradicate the child's fantasies about being his favorite teacher's son.

Faith went from weepy to annoyed in the space of a heartbeat. "I wouldn't rush into anything if I were you."

"And yet some things require quick action."

"Marriage isn't one of them."

Surprise showed clearly on Tino's face. "You believe I plan to marry?"

"Isn't that the way you plan to fix your son's desire to see me more?" Provide the little boy with a mother so he wouldn't miss the teacher he had decided he wanted in that capacity.

"It is, in fact."

Despite everything—knowing how he felt, knowing that he did not want her in his life like that—at Tino's words, unpleasant shock coursed through Faith. Somewhere deep inside, she had believed he would not go that far.

Her stomach tightened in a now familiar warning and she shot to her feet, kicking the lap blanket away. When she reached the commode, she retched. Though, since she had not been hungry earlier, she did nothing but dry heave. It hurt and it scared her. Though she knew that the cramps were in her stomach and not her womb, a tiny part of her brain kept saying it was one and the same.

Tino had come into the small room with her and she could hear water running, but she couldn't look up long enough to see what he was doing. Then a cold, damp cloth draped the nape of her neck while another one was pressed gently to her forehead. Tino rubbed her back in a soothing circular motion, crooning to her in Italian.

The heaving stopped and she found herself leaning sideways into his strength. He said nothing, just let her draw heat and comfort from his touch. She didn't know how long they remained like that—him crouching around her like a protective angel—her kneeling on the floor, but eventually she moved to stand.

He helped her, gently wiping her face with one damp cloth before tossing them both in her small sink. "Better?"

She nodded. "I don't like being sick."

"I do not imagine you do." He handed her a glass of water.

She rinsed her mouth before drinking some down. Placing the glass down by the sink, she turned to leave and weaved a bit.

Suddenly she found herself lifted in the strong arms she had been craving earlier. There was no thought to protest. She needed this. Even if it was a moment of fantasy in her rapidly failing reality.

He carried her to her minuscule bedroom, barely big enough for the double-size bed— another purchase made with hope for something that had never developed between them—and single bedside table that occupied it.

He sat her on the bed, reaching around her to arrange her pillows into a support for her back. Then he helped her to settle against them. It was all too much, too like what she secretly craved that she felt those stupid tears burning her eyes again.

Ignoring the overwrought emotions she knew were a result of pregnancy hormones, she teased, "How did you know where my bedroom was?"

"Instinct?"

She forced a laugh that came out sounding hollow rather than amused, but it was better than crying like a weakling. "Are you saying you have a homing device for beds?"

"Maybe beds belonging to you." He brushed her hair back from one side of her temple and smiled, the look almost tender.

But she knew better. "This is the only one I have."

"For the last year, almost, you have been sharing the bed in my apartment in Marsala and you have shared my bed in my family home."

"Are you trying to say those beds belong to me in some way now?" she asked, unable to completely quell her sarcasm at such a thought.

"Yes."

She gasped but could think of nothing to say in reply until she spluttered, "That's— It's *ridiculous*."

He shrugged. "We will agree to disagree."

After everything he had said? She didn't think so. "We will?" she asked in a tone she used so rarely he'd probably never heard it.

He gave her that Zen look again and nodded, as if he had no idea he was in imminent danger of being beaned upside the head with a pillow. "It is the only rational thing to do. You clearly do not need to upset yourself."

"I…" She wanted to tell him he was wrong, but she couldn't. She didn't relish the thought of more dry heaves at all. She wanted to say she didn't know what was wrong, or that she had a touch of the flu or something…anything but the truth. Only, she could not, *would* not lie.

He patted her arm. "Rest here. I will get your tea."

"Fine, but your beds don't belong to me in any way, Tino. You made that clear."

Not a single spark of irritation fluctuated his features.

What in the world was going on?

He'd gotten plenty upset over her stuffy nose, fever and headache.

So, where the heck was he with her tea?

She was on the verge of going after it herself when he walked into the small room, filling it with his presence. Why had he decided to come see her *after* they'd broken up? Even this brief visit was going to haunt her when she tried to sleep in her lonely bed at night.

He placed a steaming mug and a small plate with crackers and mild cheese on it on the table beside her bed. Then he leaned down to adjust the pillows so she could sit up more fully.

"I'm not an invalid, you know." She winced at the crabby tone to her own voice. Ashamed, she laid her hand on his wrist as he reached for the tea again. "I'm sorry. Thank you for getting my tea."

"Do not worry about it. Moodiness is to be expected." He spoke with all the patience of a man bent on humoring the woman in his life.

Only she wasn't in his life. Was she? Right now, it sure didn't feel like they'd broken up.

And she *had* been moody when she'd been

sick before. And he'd been patient. She was sure he had been the ideal husband during Maura's pregnancy. And even though he was only being so nice because he thought she was ill, she would take what she could get. "Thanks for being so understanding."

He settled onto the bed beside her, careful not to jostle and handed her the mug. "Drink."

"Bossy."

He shrugged.

She took a sip. "It's sweet." Very.

"The doctor said sugar might help with the nausea. He said the crackers and a nonpungent cheese might also help."

"What doctor?"

"The one I called."

"Overkill, Tino." But sweet. Even sweeter than the tea. She took another sip. The well-sugared beverage did seem to be helping with her upset stomach.

"Not at all. When in doubt, go to an expert."

She shook her head. "You're too funny sometimes."

"Right now I am not laughing."

No, he wasn't. He looked genuinely worried and *guilty*. "It's not your fault I got sick."

"I think it was."

"No. I…it's been like this for the past few days." That at least was pure truth, if not the entire truth.

"Only a few days. It was better before?"

"Naturally."

He examined her, as if he was trying to decide if he believed her or not. She ignored him and took a bite of cheese and cracker. Oh, that did hit the spot. Her empty stomach began to rumble for more sustenance.

"You have not eaten?"

"I wasn't hungry."

"You must take care of yourself. You cannot skip meals."

He was right, even if he didn't know how much. "I'll do better in future."

"I will see that you do."

"Right, because we spend so much time together. I mean before we broke up."

"I do not consider us broken up."

"Don't be arrogant."

"I cannot force you to stay with me, but surely

circumstances dictate a certain level of leniency on your part?"

The admission shocked her. She'd always gotten the impression that Tino thought he could make anything happen if he worked at it hard enough. She supposed his words indicated a necessary level of respect for her. But she did not get where he expected tolerance from her.

If he knew she was pregnant, that would be one thing, but there was no way he could know. She didn't show any physical signs and she hadn't told anyone but her doctor. Even if by some weird stroke of coincidence, Tino and her doctor were friends, the older man was hardly likely to chat about his patients.

No, there was no way Tino could know, but he was acting very strangely.

"Uh, Tino, you're being really odd tonight."

"You think so?" he asked.

"Yes, but, uh…that's okay. No need to explain."

"You think not?"

"No, really. We all have our moments."

"Funny, I have never been accused of having *mine* before."

"You're serious?"

"Definitely."

"You need to get out more."

"Lately I have had little excuse for getting out."

"You mean you haven't started shopping for that new wife yet?" The words came rolling off her tongue, a ball of bitterness landing between them.

"I do not need to shop."

"You already know her?" Who was it? Faith tried to think of the women Agata had mentioned, but no one came forth as a potential candidate for Tino's new wife.

"Intimately."

"You bastard." Her hand shot out in an involuntary arc that ended in a crack against his cheek. Shocked at her own actions, she nevertheless cried, "We promised each other exclusivity!"

He grabbed her hand—and examined it for damage. "Did you hurt yourself? You should not get so worked up. You are going to be sick again."

"And whose fault is that?" She meant to sound accusing, but the words came out sounding weak. Bewildered.

Because that was what she felt.

Why wasn't he furious with her?

She'd slapped him. A lump lodged in her throat, and she did her best to swallow it down without giving vent to the emotions roiling through her. She wasn't a violent person. He knew that, but she'd broken her own personal code without thought. She would have imagined he would be spitting nails in anger right now, but he was looking at her with a peculiar expression of indulgence.

"Do you know my doctor?" she asked suspiciously.

"Not that I am aware of, no."

"You don't have psychic tendencies I don't know about?"

"Definitely not."

Okay, so he couldn't possibly know about the baby. "You just admitted to cheating on me," she said, her words laced with pain she couldn't begin to suppress in her current state.

His expression zoomed to total affront in less than a second and was tempered by concern only a half a second later. "I did no such thing. I am no liar. I do not cheat."

"You lied to your mom, about us being friends." She tugged her hand out of his grip.

"I have come to realize I know too little about you to call you a true friend. I will be rectifying this in the future, however. I have already taken some steps to do so."

"You expect me to be your friend when you marry another woman?" None of this was making any sense. He could not be so cruel.

"You are being irrational. This is to be expected, but please remember what kind of man I am before you start flinging such offensive accusations."

She stared at him, totally at a loss as to what to say.

"I did not say I was going to marry another woman."

"Yes, you did." Did he think she would ever have made something so painful up in her own mind?

"I did not."

"I'm nauseous, not nuts. I know what I heard you say." And it had hurt.

"I said I planned to marry."

"Exactly."

"I did not say I planned to marry *someone else*."

He could not mean it. She shook her head. "You don't... You won't... I'm not..."

It was his turn to roll his eyes. "I do. I will. You are."

"Are you asking me to marry you?" In what she might describe as the least-romantic proposal ever. Getting her so upset she had been sick was not the way to a woman's heart.

He flinched, just slightly, but she saw it. "More informing you that I am willing to meet your terms."

Terms. A sinking feeling drained the energy from her and she fell back against the pillows. "You want me in your bed so much you are willing to marry me?"

He didn't answer.

"No. I don't believe that."

"Does it matter what my reasons are?"

"Yes."

"You need me. I need you. We need to marry." He shrugged. "My family loves you already."

She ignored the bit about his family. He hadn't been so quiescent about their affection for her before. "You need my body, not me."

"Stop overanalyzing this."

"Then tell me why. The truth."

He sighed, looking away. "You did not ask me how my mother is."

"I spoke to her on the phone tonight. I know how she is."

"You noticed her upset?"

"She's upset?" No, Faith hadn't noticed. Had she gotten so wrapped up in her own challenges, she ignored a friend in need?

"Very. She feels she betrayed you."

What? Could this night get any more unreal? "How?"

"She came by to see you today at lunch."

"I know. I wasn't home."

"She has a key to your apartment."

"Yes." She'd given it to Agata in case of an emergency. It had made Faith feel like she had someone in the world who cared enough to check on her.

"She used it."

"So?"

"Her curiosity got the better of her."

Understanding washed over Faith in a wave of despair. He *did* know she was pregnant. Everything he had done and said in the last hour now made complete and total sense. Even that bit of tenderness she'd thought she'd seen in his eyes. It had been for the flicker of life within her womb.

"You know." Her voice came out a whisper, but it was the best she could do as those pesky tears she'd been fighting since his arrival redoubled their efforts to expose her weakness.

"I do." He laid his hand on her stomach, leaving no doubt about exactly what they were discussing.

"She guessed."

"Yes."

"I knew she would if she saw the statues."

"She saw only one, but it was enough."

"And she told you?"

"When Mama is upset, she vents. My father was swimming with Giosue."

"So, she vented to you."

"*Sí.*"

"And you assumed you were the father."

"As you said, we promised exclusivity."

"You had no doubts about my integrity."

"No."

"And now you want to marry me."

"I have no choice." He took Faith's hand between both of his much larger ones. "*We* have no choice."

She shook her head.

"Be reasonable, Faith. It is the only way."

"No. It... We... There are other options."

Acute horror darkened his eyes to near black. "You would not abort our child."

"No, I wouldn't, and if you really knew me at all, *you* would know that."

"I told you that was something I planned to correct."

"Be still my heart."

"Do not mock me, Faith."

She took a fortifying sip of tea. "I don't have to marry you."

"You would deny my child his father?"

"Sheesh, Tino, you are so all or nothing. First you think I'm going to have an abortion and now you think I'm going to refuse you parental rights."

"Are you?"

So much for his trust in her integrity. "No."

"So, marry me."

"There are other choices."

"None that are as good."

"Right, because marriage for the sake of a baby is going to create a family that baby is going to love being raised in."

"We are compatible—there is nothing wrong with this picture."

"You left out one little aspect that is supposed to exist in marriage."

"What?"

Could he really be that dense? "Love, Tino. I'm talking about love."

"We care for each other."

So much that this was only the second time he had ever been to her apartment. "It's not enough."

"It is. Many people marry with less."

"I loved Taylish and he loved me." Maybe they hadn't felt the same kind of love for each other, but the love had been there.

Tino's jaw hardened. "I loved Maura, but she is gone as is your Taylish. *We* are here now. That is all that matters."

"Not even. You were completely unwilling to entertain the idea of marriage before."

"I did not know you carried my child."

Did he have any concept of the kind of damage his words were doing to her heart? Of course not. Love had not come up between them until she asked for it. He couldn't begin to understand how much his attitude hurt.

She hunched her shoulders, hugging herself, but the cold was seeping into her heart, anyway. "I knew it."

"Knew what?"

"That if I told you I was pregnant, you would insist on marriage. Do you even begin to see how feudal-lord your thinking is?"

"I am a Grisafi." As if that said it all.

"Well, I'm not and I'm not sure I want to be one, either."

His already-tense jaw developed a tic, but his voice remained even. "My mother's heart would be broken to hear you say that."

"I wouldn't be marrying your mother."

"I should hope not." He laughed, the sound low and sexy despite the topic of their conversation—or maybe because of it.

Marriage to Tino. A dream come true for all the wrong reasons.

He put his arm over her thighs in a proprietary gesture she did not miss the meaning of. "You say there are other options."

"There are."

"Name them."

"I didn't say you were going to like them," she felt the need to warn.

"If they do not include marriage between us, I think that is safe to assume." The Zen tone of ultimate patience was back.

"They don't."

He just waited.

"Fine, but I want to point out that I'm in no condition to argue."

Amusement flickered in his dark gaze. "I did not notice you having any trouble doing so up to this point."

"I mean it, Tino. I've had my limit of upset for the evening."

His expression went ultraserious. "I will not distress you again."

She nodded, knowing full well she was taking advantage. But the truth was? She *didn't* want to argue. Her emotional reserves had been in the negative totals for weeks now.

"I could go back to America and raise the baby there. You could visit."

She waited for the explosion, but it never came. He simply sat there staring at her.

"Nothing to say?" she had to ask.

He shook his head, and it was then she realized his jaw was clenched tight.

"I don't want to do that."

"Good." He bit the word out, but the sense of relief he felt was palpable.

"I was just pointing out that it was an option." And trying to hurt him back a little for

the pain he had dealt her? The thought morti-
fied her. She was not that kind of person.

"Noted."

"I want to stay in Sicily," she said quickly,
wanting him to know right away she wasn't
going to hurt him with the baby. "I love it here
and I want our child to grow up knowing its
family. The Grisafis are all he or she has in the
way of extended relatives, and they're wonderful people to boot." She tried a tentative smile.

He did not return it. "So, marry me."

She wanted to, badly, but not merely for the
sake of the baby. "I could stay here."

Appalled was the only word to describe his
look. "In *this* apartment?"

"It is kind of small for a baby." She bit her lip,
wincing when it drew blood. "I could find a
bigger place."

"You can move into the family home."

"I considered that." She had, after examining
every other alternative—living with the Grisafis
was the only way she could give the baby the
life it deserved. Not monetarily—she was set in
that regard—but the daily access to people who

would love the baby and the baby would grow to love. Including its father.

That didn't mean he would have access to her. That point was not negotiable. But she wanted her baby to have a family. The pain of growing up without her parents had dulled with time, but never disappeared. She wanted her baby to have its grandparents, its brother, its father close by—to live in a home filled with love and people who would enrich the baby's life.

The Grisafi home was big enough to accommodate her and the baby in a set of rooms that would be much like having her own apartment. And yet there would be easy and consistent access to familial ties important to the baby's well-being.

"So, you will marry me."

"That's not what I said. I can live in your family home without being your wife. It's definitely big enough."

"Why would you deny me my rightful place in my child's life?"

"I will not do that. You will be named on the

birth certificate, the baby can have the Grisafi name."

"But you do not want it."

She was about to say no, but she could not force the word from her mouth. So she shook her head.

"Why, Faith? When you wanted marriage before I knew?"

"That's exactly why."

"I do not understand."

"I think you do."

"You feel slighted because I will marry you for the baby's sake and not your own."

"Yes."

"That is childish thinking, Faith." Not, *I care about you, too*. Not, *It's not the way it looks*. No, just an accusation of immaturity.

Faith's resolve not to be pressured into anything doubled. "Believe what you like, but I am not running to the courthouse for a quickie marriage."

His bark of laughter was mocking. "As if my mother would allow such a thing."

Faith just glared at him.

"You will move in, though?"

"I said it was something I was considering. That it was an option."

"It is the best option you have suggested so far."

"Actually, you suggested it."

"But you had considered it?"

"Yes."

"Favorably?"

"Yes."

"So, what is stopping you from agreeing?"

"I'm not sure I want to live in the same house as you," she answered honestly.

He reeled back as if struck. "You hate me so much."

"I don't hate you at all, but I'm not sure this is what is best for us."

"It is best for the baby and that is all that matters."

"On that point we agree."

"So, you will move in."

"You're stubborn."

"Very."

She sighed.

He took it as acquiescence, if the grim satisfaction on his face could be believed. "How soon?"

"I haven't agreed, Tino," she pointed out. "If I decide that's the best course of action, and provided your parents approve the idea, I would move in after the baby is born."

"You need looking after *now*. Tonight proves that."

"Tonight I thought you were telling me that the father of my unborn child wanted to marry another woman. *A suitable Sicilian woman.*"

"Stress induced your stomach upset?"

"Yes, I think so."

"We will have to make sure you are not distressed in any way from this point forward."

"I would appreciate that." If she had known it would be so easy, she would have played the illness card earlier. Exhaustion overcame her, like it did sometimes lately. "I'm tired," she said, knowing he had to be able to see it. "We can talk more about this at a later time."

"Very well."

She reached up and brushed his cheek,

needing to say one last thing before he left for the night. "I'm sorry I slapped you."

"I forgive you."

"Thank you," she slurred as sleep overtook her.

CHAPTER TEN

FAITH had fallen asleep. Just like that.

Thirty seconds later and her breathing had already leveled out into true somnolence. It always amazed him how she could do that, though the only other times he'd seen it was after they had made love. They hadn't done so tonight.

Yet, here she was—sleeping. Dark bruises marred the lovely skin below her eyes. Her pregnancy was taking it out of her. It bothered him to see her looking so frail. Was she taking her vitamins? Had she gone to a doctor? There were so many questions he needed answered, but she wasn't going to be satisfying his need to know right now.

It wouldn't be until morning, if he had his way and she slept the night through. He was careful not to jostle her unduly as he removed her clothes to increase her comfort. He could not help but stop and look at the changes her pregnancy had already wrought on her beautiful body.

With near reverence, he cataloged each one. Her breasts were slightly bigger and the aureoles had darkened. She had an exhausted air about her, but she glowed too, her skin reflecting an overall abundance of health. He could see no evidence of the baby within in the curve of her belly. It was no bigger.

The need to touch was intense and he carefully placed his hand over her lower abdomen, a sense of awe permeating him. It might not look different, but although he might be being fanciful, he would swear he could feel the presence of his child in her womb. Usually when he massaged her tummy, the flesh was soft with feminine give. Now below the silken skin, it felt hard, solid. Amazing.

She made a soft noise and turned on her side to curl into her pillow.

He found himself smiling, but then frowned in thought. He knew she expected him to leave, but he wasn't going to. He'd agreed not to argue; he hadn't agreed to vacate her apartment, leaving her alone, with no one to care for her needs.

He flipped out his cell and called home to tell his parents he would not be returning tonight. Thankfully, his father answered, so Tino was not subjected to a barrage of questions when he said he would not be home that night. His mother tried calling ten minutes later, but he let the call go to voice mail. He wasn't ready to speak to her yet.

He and Faith had some explaining to do and Tino was determined to do it on his own agenda and in his own way.

Faith woke up with a sense of well-being that had been missing for the past several weeks. The sense that she had been held in strong arms all night long tickled at her conscience, but she dismissed it as leftover dreams from the night before. Just like so many other mornings.

Her stomach was slightly upset, but nothing like the night before. Memories of Tino's visit beset her, but she wasn't ready to deal with the implications of his discovery. Not if she wanted to keep a handle on the physical side effects of her pregnancy. She would keep her mind blank, and if she moved slowly, hopefully she could avoid anything beyond the mild nausea.

She started with opening her eyes and orienting herself to her surroundings. The first thing she noticed was the mug of tea on her bedside table. Steam was coming from it. The cheese and crackers on the plate beside it looked fresh, as did the grapes accompanying it.

Trying to make sense of the fresh libations, she sat up carefully. No matter how curious she was, she wasn't going to jostle her queasy tummy.

As the sheets slid against her skin, she realized she was naked.

Completely and totally.

"Tino!"

Despite the evidence of his presence, she was still shocked when he came rushing in. And looking too damn good in nothing but his boxers, too. "Are you all right, *piccola madre mia?* Did you try the tea? It should settle your stomach. Do you need help to the bathroom?"

The babbling would be endearing if,

well…maybe it was endearing regardless, but still. And calling her his little mother, that was…it was…she didn't know what it was. Cute? Maybe. "What are you doing here?"

"Caring for you, as you can see." He swept his hand out to indicate the mug and plate of food.

"I meant what are you doing here at all?"

"I spent the night."

"In my bed?"

"Your small sofa is much too short. Besides, you might have needed me in the night."

Once she got used to the fact he was there, with her, in her apartment, she had no problem believing he had spent the night in her bed. And while she knew it should bother her, it didn't. It made her feel cared for, darn it. He hadn't made sexual overtures after all, he'd just been there for her.

The sensation of having been held throughout the night was not her imagination, nor had it been yet another hollow dream. The fact that she wanted it so badly made her cranky. "You said you were leaving."

"I did not."

"You—"

"I promised not to argue with you last night."

Right, and she had assumed that meant he would accede to her wishes. "You are sneaky, Tino."

"I prefer to think of it as resourceful." He gave her the smile that had been melting her heart for almost a year. "You should drink your tea and eat. The doctor said it would be most helpful if you partake before getting out of bed."

"Taylish used to have soda crackers and a glass of flat Seven-Up ready for me in the morning." She sighed, looking around her small room. "I'd forgotten."

"Would you prefer that?" Tino asked with a flat voice. "Only the doctor recommended these items."

"This is fine."

He nodded and left the room.

Mentally shrugging at his strange behavior, she drank her tea. She'd eaten the crackers and cheese and several of the grapes as well before Tino returned. They did help. She felt almost normal, certainly not in any risk for a hasty trip to the bathroom to void her stomach.

Tino was still wearing nothing more than his

boxer shorts, a luxurious emerald-green silk she wanted to touch. Which was really, really stupid, but true all the same.

Her nipples tightened—aching a little because they were tender from the hormonal changes in her body—and reminding her of her total nudity beneath the sheet and blanket. "You undressed me last night. While I was sleeping."

"If I had done it while you were awake, I am sure the outcome would have been quite different." He gave her a heavy-lidded look that sent sparks of arousal straight to her core.

"No." She shook her head in further denial, trying to convince them both that what he was suggesting was not an option.

He sat beside her and cupped her nape, his hand warm and big against her neck. "Are you sure about that?"

"We can't. Tino, no sex." Though her body was aching for the feel of his.

"Why?" His expression grew worried and his entire body tensed. "Has your doctor identified a problem with your pregnancy."

"No," she admitted, knowing she was going to sound paranoid. "He says that I'm healthy and so is the baby." He'd also said that the vast majority of miscarriages in the first trimester could not have been avoided. It was simply a matter of an unviable pregnancy ending itself.

She wasn't that clinically detached.

"So, why no sex?"

"Do you know the risk of miscarriage in the first trimester, Tino?"

"No."

"It's 12.5 percent. The number is probably higher because some women miscarry before they even realize they are pregnant, but one in eight known pregnancies end in miscarriage in the first trimester. But even if it was only one in a million, I wouldn't do anything to risk it."

"Certainly, if making love increases the risk, we will not do so. I am surprised Maura's doctor never said anything." Tino sounded angered by that fact.

Faith had to be truthful. "Um, there's actually no evidence to suggest that normal sexual activity increases the risk of an early trimester miscarriage."

"But you are still afraid of taking the risk."

"Yes."

"So, we will abstain," he said with the air of a man making a great sacrifice if not with pleasure, without recrimination. "It will make for an interesting wedding night, though."

"We aren't getting married." At least not right now.

"We shall see." He stood up. "Now I believe it is time to ready ourselves for the day. Do you need help in the shower?"

"I'm pregnant, not an invalid, Tino. I can bathe myself."

"That is probably for the best. Prolonged exposure to your wet, naked body would not be good for my self-control."

"You always talk like I'm some sort of femme fatale."

"Perhaps that is because you are death to the control I exercise over my libido."

She laughed, feeling pleased when she knew she shouldn't. After all, they were no longer a couple. But, like the night before, she had a hard time remembering that, when it felt so right to be with him.

Tino dressed while Faith was in the shower, and then he made a couple of business calls while she was getting ready. Anything to keep himself from going into her small bedroom and ravishing her body.

For some reason, Faith feared miscarriage. He refused to add to those fears, no matter how difficult it might be to abstain from intimacy with her luscious body. He had to admit, he had no idea that miscarriage was so prevalent in the first trimester.

He did a quick web search on his PDA while he waited for Faith to come out of the bedroom, and discovered some interesting facts.

When she came out, she was wearing a flowing sundress the same peacock blue as her eyes in a halter style that tied around her neck. The deep vee of the neckline accentuated her burgeoning curves, but the dress looked comfortable, as well. Its empire waistline had no binding around her tummy, he noticed.

It would look even more amazing once her stomach started to protrude with the baby. He could not wait.

"Did you know that the risk of miscarriage drops to less than one percent after the first trimester and that there are *no* studies linking normal sexual activity to the loss of the baby at all?"

She stopped and stared at him for a half second and then laughed. "Tino, you are too much. Did you call the doctor again while I was in the shower?"

Chagrined at the thought that doing so might have carried more weight with her, he shook his head. "Web research."

"I didn't realize you knew the password to my computer."

"I don't. I used my PDA."

"Trust you to go right to the heart of the matter, and yes, I did know that. I told you as much, remember?"

"I didn't know if you realized it held true throughout your pregnancy."

"I did."

"Good."

She just shook her head and went to sit on the love seat she'd used the night before. This time he sat down beside her and pulled her legs into his lap, starting to massage one of her feet.

She gave him a shocked little stare. "Why are you doing that?"

"To make you feel good."

"But...I'm not exactly huge with child and have aching feet yet, Tino."

"So, I am getting some practice in. If you do not like it, I will stop."

She glared. "Don't you dare. It feels wonderful."

He smiled, feeling smug. Faith had always loved a good foot rub. "Now, tell me why you are so afraid of losing this baby."

The look of ecstasy on her face changed to one of deep sorrow tinged with very real fear. "I lose the people I love, Tino. Every single one. I'm not taking any risks with this baby."

"You have not lost my mother...or my son." He didn't mention himself, because in truth, he wasn't sure she loved him. Even when she had asked him if he could love her, he hadn't known if she had those kinds of feelings for him, or was asking in the hopes of building something in the future.

"If you had your way, neither of them would be in my life."

"That is not true."

"You were angry when you found out I was Gio's teacher, that your mom is my friend."

"I was shocked—it made me respond badly—but I would not take them from your life. Even if you were not pregnant with my child." And he realized that given the choice, he would not have prevented Faith from forming the attachments with his family that she had.

She needed them.

"I believe you. I don't know why. I shouldn't, but I do."

"I am glad. I have never wished ill on you."

"I know." She reached out and brushed her fingertips down his arm.

It sent chills through him, but he ignored the stirrings of desire and said, "So you have not lost everyone you love."

"Every chance I had at family has been snatched from me, Tino." The remembered agony on her face was enough to unman him. "First my parents, then the one foster home I felt like I belonged. They were hoping to adopt a baby, and when the baby came, they let me go."

"That is terrible."

She shrugged, but her pain was there for him to see. "When I lost Taylish and our baby…" Tears filled her eyes and then slid down her cheeks while she tried to compose herself to continue. Finally she choked out, "I figured I must not be meant to have a family."

"I understand why you might feel that way." And it broke his heart for her. "But you must realize it is an irrational conclusion to draw. Though you have suffered more tragedy than any woman should have to, you are still alive— you have much to give to a family and much to receive from one." He took the hand still resting on his arm and kissed her palm, squeezing her fingers tightly. "You are my family now, Faith."

She pulled her hand away, with apparent reluctance, but did it all the same. "No, I'm not. If I manage to deliver this baby, *then* I'll have a family—someone who belongs to me." More tears and a final choking whisper, "Someone I belong to."

Her words sliced at his heart, leaving wounds he refused to dwell on in the midst of her sharing such a personal pain. "Marry me and you will have a ready-made son, mother, father and assorted aunts, uncles and cousins."

She shook her head, her eyes telling him she did not believe. "I won't have *you,* will I, Tino?"

"Of course you will have me. I will be your husband." He could not understand how that could mean not having him.

She just shook her head.

He couldn't stand it any longer. He pulled her into his lap, wrapping his arms around her. "I cannot imagine how you have survived losing the people you have. You are a strong, beautiful woman, Faith. A woman I would be proud to call my wife."

He could feel the edges cracking around his promise to Maura, but he could not pull back. Not in the face of Faith's sorrow.

"You only want to marry me for the baby's sake."

"And for your sake and yes, for my sake. I want you, Faith, and maybe you don't think that is very important, but I have never craved a woman physically the way I do you."

"Not even Maura?"

"No." It hurt to admit and shamed him, but Faith deserved the truth. As much as he had loved his wife, she had not elicited the same sense of soul-deep need for physical oneness that the woman in his arms did.

"I don't want to lose any more family," Faith said in a pained undertone.

"You will not lose this baby. You will not lose me."

"You can't know that."

"And you are not a person who gives up on life because of fear, or you would have given up already." He held her tightly to him. "There is also the baby to consider. We can give her more stability as a married couple, *cara,* than simply living as house mates."

"Her?"

"I can think of nothing I would like better than a daughter who takes after her spirited and beautiful mama."

"Don't say things like that."

"I cannot help it."

"But…"

"I am not only thinking of the baby." He had to convince Faith to marry him.

"Who else?"

"My mother. You carry her grandbaby inside you. She will not be happy if you do not marry me."

"Your mother knows you better than I do, she will understand."

Tino managed a laugh at the implied insult, despite the heavy emotions surrounding them. "No, she will take it quite personally and will be heartbroken if you refuse to make yourself her daughter-in-law."

"I cannot marry you because it will make Agata happy."

"What about Giosue?"

Faith flinched, her beautiful blue eyes clouding. "You said he deserves someone better than me."

"I did not."

"You did. You want to give him a *Sicilian* stepmother, so he will have someone at least that much like his real mother."

Hearing his own reasoning quoted back to him was not pleasant in this instance. How could he have said that to Faith, even if he had believed it at the time? Once again that morning, he felt shame. "My son does not agree. He does not want a traditional Sicilian woman for a stepmother. He wants a free-spirited artist who loves children enough to teach them though it is a mixed blessing for her because being around those children reminds her of what she has lost."

Faith buried her face in his chest. "You said you do not know me."

"Maybe I know you better than either of us thinks." That thought was *not* an unpleasant one. "Can you do it?"

She did not ask what he meant, but he explained anyway. "Can you marry for the sake of our child, for the sake of my mother and your dear friend, for the sake of Giosue's happiness, a little boy you already love? For the sake of your own inner strength that sees beauty and joy in a world that has already taken so much from you? Can you marry me because it is the right thing to do?"

She swallowed and spoke. "Ask me again in two weeks." Her voice was barely above a whisper, as if forcing the words out had been difficult.

"Why two weeks?" he asked, rubbing her back and marveling anew at her resiliency.

He had never known another person like Faith. She amazed him, never more so than today after he heard the short version of her life story.

"My first trimester will be over."

"What has that got to do with anything?"

She sat up and looked away from him, her gaze going to the view out the sunroom's floor-to-ceiling windows. "You only want to marry me because I am pregnant with your child. If that pregnancy ends, you would resent the fact we had married because of it."

"What is all this negative talk? You are not

going to lose our baby. If you want to go without sex until you feel it is safe, I will not argue. But I refuse to consider the possibility of future miscarriage in making the decision about marriage. You are not going to lose us."

She was looking at him now, her eyes wide but no longer spilling over with tears. "You can't promise that."

"I can promise that baby, or no baby, I expect to marry you."

"No."

"Yes."

"That makes no sense."

"It does to me."

"It's an obligation thing." Horror cascaded over her features. "You pity me."

He laughed. He could not help it. It was not a sound of happy amusement, but a grim one. "You are too strong to pity."

"I'm not. I'm scared to death. That makes me a coward. I don't want to tempt fate."

"You are no coward."

"I don't know how we jumped to talk of marriage. Last night we were negotiating whether or not I'm going to move into the Grisafi villa."

"I go after what I want."

"And what you want is me to marry you?" She sounded disbelieving.

"Believe it." He tilted her chin with the edge of his hand, so their eyes continued to meet. "You are living scared and that is no way to live."

"Says you."

Instead of continuing to argue with her, he kissed her. It wasn't a passionate, let's-make-love kiss, but a tender salute of comfort. Then, leaning his head against hers, he spoke. "Faith, I want you to live up to your name. I want you to have hope in the future. I want you believe in the family we can make together."

"I don't know if I can."

"I believe in you."

She took a shuddering breath. "I want to show you something."

"Whatever you need."

She stood and he did, as well, wondering what she felt he needed to see. She was his, even if she did not yet acknowledge that fact. And the presence of their baby in her womb meant that no matter what promises he had made, the need to make her a permanent part of his life superseded them now.

He would not break the final promise and allow Faith to replace Maura in his heart, but he would spend the rest of his life proving to Faith that marriage to him was not a mistake. He had no doubts he would convince her of it.

She might not be in love with him, but she loved his mother and his son. And she loved teaching at the primary school. She would not be able to keep that job if she insisted on keeping a single status while pregnant. This was Sicily, not the more liberal UK or America.

He might not agree with all the cultural norms of his country, but he wasn't above taking advantage of them when he needed to.

Faith would marry him.

She stopped in front of a covered statue and met his eyes with hers. "You didn't look."

"No."

"Weren't you curious?"

"Very."

"But you respected my privacy."

"*Si.*" Unlike his mother. But this one time he could give thanks for her excessive curiosity. With her pessimistic views regarding her pregnancy, she would probably have waited to tell him until she was inches from giving birth—if then.

Faith's fingers were on the cloth, but she had not lifted it, though he assumed that was her plan. "You didn't think undressing me compromised that?"

"I have mapped every centimeter of your naked body with my eyes, my fingers…my tongue. There are no secrets between us in that regard."

"And if I did not want you undressing me?"

"It has never bothered you before."

"But we broke up, Tino."

"Did we?" He stepped closer until they were sharing breathing space. "Or were we on hiatus while you worked out best when and how to tell me of our child?"

For he had no doubt she had planned to do so. He remembered comments she had made when they spoke of commitment that had made no sense at the time, but looking back had ominous import.

She looked chagrined, but did not answer.

"Even if I had been looking to marry again— which I was not—you would not have allowed me to do so without informing me of our child's existence, would you?"

"No."

"Nor would I have ever let you walk away, but admit it—you were biding your time before we reconciled."

"I wasn't." She bit her lip and sighed, her blue eyes troubled. "You seem to forget you were the one who was so adamantly opposed to marriage *to me.*"

"If I could go back and change my responses to you in that regard, I would." Because even without the baby, he now admitted he could never have let Faith walk out of his life. He wasn't proud of his weakness, but he would not lie to himself about it, either.

"I am arrogant. I admit it, but truth is truth. You have never stopped belonging to me and vice versa."

"We were casual lovers, Tino. Bed partners. Not a couple." Bitterness and confusion laced her voice in equal measure. "We didn't belong to each other."

"That is not how I see it."

"Oh, really? That's why you refused my calls for two weeks while you were in New York." That was his Faith, still fragile from her admissions, but ready to speak her mind regardless.

"Yes."

Blue eyes went wide in shock. "What?"

"I was not comfortable with the depth our relationship had attained, and I attempted to retrench to a less emotionally intimate position." He took a deep breath and prepared to speak words that rarely passed his lips. "I am truly sorry that hurt you."

"I…" She looked lost for words, but then visibly regrouped. "It must have worked, or you would not have denied our friendship to your mother."

"You know that is not true." They would lay this to rest once and for all. "I explained why I said what I did, and if it makes you feel any better, I learned to regret it." Deeply.

"The big bad, business tycoon was afraid of his mother. Very convincing, Tino."

Just about as convincing as his Faith giving in to sarcasm. "Mocking me will not change the truth of our circumstances."

She sighed, as if her anger was deflating. "I know that."

"We belong to each other. My idiocy and your intransigency cannot change that. Admit it."

CHAPTER ELEVEN

FAITH shook her head. "You never give up, do you?"

"No."

"You are a piece of work, Valentino Grisafi."

"If you mean 'a piece of work' like those you create, I will take that as a compliment."

"Thank you."

"You are a very talented artist."

"I hope you continue to think so after seeing these pieces."

And then she showed him, one after another. Each one was a pregnant woman in a different situation and varying stages of pregnancy, from barely pregnant to one where the woman looked as if she was ready to give imminent birth to twins.

The most striking thing about the collection

was the wealth of emotion it expressed—and elicited. There was one woman in a state of misery, clearly on the edge of losing her child. There was another who glowed with such joy it choked him. Another was a grouping, a man, a woman and a child. The man and child had their hands on the protruding belly of the mother-to-be. One of her more abstract pieces, their features were blank and the sex of the child was not clear. But Tino was sure it was a little boy and that both man and boy wore grins on their faces.

He was certain the statue represented something Faith hoped for, something Tino was determined he and Giosue could give her. Acceptance. And family.

He reached out to touch the woman who looked on the verge of final tragedy. "Is this how you feel right now?"

"Sometimes."

He pulled the emotionally fragile woman to him and kissed the top of her silky red curls, inhaling her scent and trying to imbue her with his confidence. "You will not lose this baby."

"I have to believe that, or I would go crazy."

"But you are still afraid." He rubbed her back, loving the feel of her smaller body so close to his.

"Terrified."

"You are also happy."

"Ecstatic."

Something inside him settled when she admitted that. "You want the baby."

"Very, very, *very* much." She hugged him tight as if that was the only way to express the depth of her feelings on the matter.

"Three *very*s. That *is* a lot." And he was glad.

"Yes."

He drew back a little, not pulling from her embrace but far enough that he could tilt her head and let their gazes meet. "But you do not want the father."

"That is not what I said." She pouted, just like she did when he told her it was time to go home after a night of lovemaking.

Remembering those occasions now caused an internal wince. "Certain things can be inferred."

"No, they can't."

He leaned back against her worktable, tugging

her with him so she ended up plastered against him. "Oh, really?"

She seemed disinclined to move, snuggling against him trustingly. "Yes. I just…"

"What?"

"I told you…I don't want to tempt fate." She dipped her head, so he could not see her face.

He could not help himself from cupping her bottom and massaging it. Her curves were so damn enticing to him. "Why not try trusting in Providence instead of worrying about fate?"

"I never thought I could lose my parents."

"You did."

"Yes and believe me when I tell you that I was sure Taylish and the baby were my shot at a family. A family I was positive could not be taken from me. I knew he would never leave me."

"Then he did."

"It wasn't his fault, but it wasn't mine either, and I was alone again."

"Look at me."

She tilted her head back, her peacock-blue eyes shiny with emotion.

He felt like he'd been kicked in the gut with that look. "You are not alone now."

"You don't think?"

"I know. And so should you. Even without the baby, you had my mother, my son, your friends…me."

"Did I have you, Tino?"

"More than any other woman since Maura's death." That fact was not a comfortable one for him, but it was something Faith deserved to know.

"You aren't happy about that," she said perceptively.

"If I could choose any woman on the planet to have awakened such emotions in me, it would have been you." He could wish he had not slighted his own honor, but never that another woman had been the cause.

He did not believe any other woman *could* have been.

"I don't know what to say."

"Say you will marry me." He dropped his hand to palm her hard stomach. "I need you to believe in the future, if not for my sake, then for the baby's."

"But—"

He lifted his other hand and pressed a finger to her lips. "No buts."

"I want to believe."

"Then do."

"It's not that easy."

"I know, but you must try."

"My first pregnancy was ectopic." The words were bald and emotionless, but he could feel more remembered pain radiating from her.

For a moment his vocal chords were paralyzed with grief for her. "You lost your first baby?"

"Yes."

"I had read that a tubal pregnancy could be very dangerous for the mother."

She nodded, her expression matter-of-fact. "I almost died."

"And you still risked pregnancy again." He was not sure that as her husband, he would have had the strength to allow her to do so.

Taylish had either been a saint or an idiot. Tino knew which one he preferred to believe.

"Absolutely."

He gave a hollow, self-deprecating laugh. "Do you know? I thought you did not want children."

"I did not think it would ever be an option. I believed I would not be able to get pregnant again. Tay and I had to resort to a fertility specialist before I could get pregnant the second time."

"So, this baby is a miracle."

"Yes."

Joy settled inside him. "Believe in the strength of that miracle, Faith."

"Meeting you was a miracle, Tino."

"What?" He could not accept she had said that.

"Wanting you shocked me. I had not expected to ever have another intimate relationship with a man." She rubbed her cheek against his chest as if she needed the contact.

She had been that in love with Taylish? Certainly, the couple had not had an intensely satisfying sexual relationship. Not like he and Faith did. Her reaction to the pleasure she felt when they first made love indicated she'd never experienced something like it before. "But you desired me."

"Yes."

He squeezed her close. "I want you, too, *bella mia.*"

"I know." There was a smile in her voice, and she moved a little to let him feel that she could feel the evidence pressing against her belly.

"So marry me."

She laughed softly as if amused, not frustrated, by his persistence. "It's not that simple."

"It can be if you let it."

"You're so stubborn, Tino."

"You love that about me."

She was silent for a count of five full seconds, then she kissed him through his shirt, right over his heart. "Maybe."

Faith spent the morning working, feeling inspired and better than she had in weeks. Every brush with her palette knife was perfect, every gentle manipulation of the clay with her fingers resulting in just the effect she was looking for.

A loud beeping from her small alarm told her it was time to start getting ready for lunch with Agata. She was washing the clay from her hands in the kitchen sink when someone knocked.

Thinking Agata had decided to come by and pick her up instead of meeting at the restaurant as planned, Faith dried her hands and swung the door open.

To a frowning Tino. "You did not ask who it was. There is no peephole on your door. How did you know it was me?"

"Sheesh, arrogant much? I didn't know it was you."

"I believed we already established that that is a Grisafi family trait." He bent down and kissed her, his lips lingering just long enough to make it the kiss of a lover and not a typically warm Sicilian greeting. "If you did not know it was me, why did you open the door?"

"I thought it was your mother."

"I was under the impression your plans were to meet at the restaurant for lunch."

Faith didn't remember telling him the details of her lunch appointment, but just like with her first pregnancies, her short-term memory was just a tad compromised. "I thought she might have arrived in town early and decided to pick me up."

"But you did not know."

"Clearly not. After all, I was wrong, wasn't I?"

"And yet you opened the door."

"Is there a point to this interrogation?"

"A point?" He stepped inside and shut the door. "Yes, there is a point. I could have been anyone."

"But you weren't."

"Nevertheless, such behavior is reckless."

"Reckless? Opening the door?"

"Opening your door when you do not know who is on the other side puts your safety at needless risk."

"What are you? The arbiter of in-home security for pregnant women?"

"This has nothing to do with your pregnancy."

She believed him. "You look so fierce, Tino."

"Do not make fun of my concern for you, Faith. I should have visited you here long before this. No doubt, you have been behaving in a similar fashion all this time."

"This is Sicily, Tino, not New York City. I can

open the door without worrying the person on the other side is set on robbing me."

"Or worse? I do not think so. Marsala is not such a small city as all that, and there are plenty of tourists with intentions you cannot begin to be certain of."

"Overprotective alert, Tino."

"I think not. Common sense is not overprotective behavior." But color burnished along his chiseled cheekbones.

"I like this side of you," she decided.

"Good. I am unlikely to change."

"That I believe." She grinned, then frowned. "Um, not that I want to kick you out or anything." She so didn't, no matter how little sense that attitude made. "But I'm supposed to meet your mother for lunch in less than an hour and I need to get ready. Was there something in particular you needed?"

"I am horning in on your lunch with my mother."

"What? Why?"

"You have decided to tell her about the baby, yes?"

"Yes." And she was more than a little nervous about doing so.

"As much as we both adore my mother, I am certain you could use my moral support."

"That's really sweet." Man, when he decided to take down the barriers, they crumbled with a crash. She was still glowing from the things he'd said when he'd been trying to convince her to marry him. Going back over the conversation had filled her with renewed hope and dead certainty that no matter what he had said before, Tino *wanted* to be with *her*.

She already knew she wanted to be with him. But maybe not this afternoon. "Won't your presence be suspect? Your mom isn't dumb, she's bound to guess there's more between us than a casual acquaintance."

"I am sure she drew that conclusion when I ran from the house without a word after she told me she thought you were pregnant."

"You didn't."

"I did."

"Tino!"

"I know. I was not thinking, *bella mia*."

"I didn't want to tell anyone I was pregnant until my first trimester was over," Faith lamented.

"What is done is done."

"Is that a Sicilian proverb?"

He grinned and kissed the tip of her nose. "I believe it is a universal one."

"I suppose." She headed to her bedroom. "I need to change my clothes."

He followed her.

"Tino, I'm getting dressed."

"So?"

"You really don't recognize personal boundaries, do you?"

"You wish to have a wider personal boundary as my wife than you have had as my lover?" He sounded confused and not a little upset.

"We're not married."

"Not yet, but it will happen."

"I haven't said yes." But she would. She loved him and now that she knew his feelings for her had always run deeper than he'd wanted to admit or acknowledge even to himself, she wasn't going to let him go.

He wasn't the only stubborn, possessive one in their relationship.

"You will."

"You are so sure?"

"I cannot allow myself to consider the alternative." And for just a brief moment, her Sicilian tycoon looked as vulnerable as any male on the planet. "For now I will be happy if you admit we are still a couple."

"Were we ever a *couple*?"

"We had our limits on our relationship, but that does not mean we were not together."

"Limits you set."

"I acknowledge it."

"You seem to have dumped them with efficient speed." And she was loving that reality.

"Circumstances change."

"Like finding out I'm pregnant with your baby."

"Believe it or do not, but the walls I imposed between us would have crumpled when you dumped me, regardless of your reason for doing so."

"I do believe it." Did he love her? She didn't have the guts to ask and risk getting shot down again, but the possibility warmed her heart as surely as her baby did. "So, you do admit that I dumped you, regardless of the reasons why?"

Pain darkened his expression for just a moment. "*Si.*"

"Then I can admit that we are a couple."

Gorgeous white teeth flashed in a smile that turned her inside out.

He watched as she pulled off her clay-spattered jeans and top, his gaze going hot and hungry when her almost nude body was revealed.

"You're not wearing a bra." His voice was hoarse and his hand made an abortive move to touch her.

She smiled. "No sex, remember."

"How could I forget?"

"You look like you're in danger of doing so."

"I am not, but you would not deny me what pleasure I can have, would you?"

"You are going to get yourself all revved up with nowhere to go." Though knowing he still wanted her so much was nice. Really nice to know, in fact.

He laughed. "I think a tiny part of you enjoys knowing that."

"I think you may be right."

She turned to grab some clothes from the closet, bending to get the gold and white Roca Wear sandals she wanted to wear with her white sheath dress.

He groaned.

She let her lips curve in a smile because he could not see. "You sure you're going to survive this."

"If Taylish could stand the abstinence, so can I."

"Ohh, competitive. You don't have to be. Tay and I didn't stop making love during either of my pregnancies."

Silence for a full five seconds. "I'll wait for you in the studio." He turned and left the room without another word.

She blinked, not sure what had happened there. One minute she'd been teasing him with her body, positive they were both enjoying it. And the next, he was gone.

He was quiet on the way to the restaurant to meet his mother, too.

"Tino," she said when they pulled up in front of the trattoria. "Is something wrong?"

"What could be wrong?"

"That's what I want to know."

He simply shrugged and got out of the car, coming around to open her door and help her to her feet. He kept his hand on the small of her back as they walked into the restaurant.

Agata was already seated at a table for four; Rocco was across from her.

She smiled at their approach. "Hello, Faith. My son. Why am I not surprised to see you as well?"

"Because you are intelligent enough to add two and two and get four. I, on the other hand, am a little shocked you brought Papa along without warning Faith first."

"Why, am I some ogre my soon-to-be daughter-in-law should need forewarning of my presence?"

"Do not be melodramatic, Papa."

Tino looked down at her to see how she was taking this development and she gave him and then his parents a reassuring smile. "I'm very happy to see you, Rocco."

"And I am very pleased to be expecting a new grandchild."

Tino didn't give her a chance to answer, but pulled her chair out for her. She sat down, glad there was already water at her place. She took a sip and wondered how best to break it to the older couple that she had not yet agreed to marry Tino.

"Faith has not consented to become my wife," Tino said bluntly, taking care of that little detail for her.

"You have not asked her?" Rocco asked in clear censure.

Tino waited to answer until he had taken his own seat at the table. Then he gave his father a look that would make most cringe. "Naturally, I have asked her. She turned me down."

"Flat?" Agata asked in a faint voice, her shock palpable.

Faith glared at Tino. So much for supporting her during this conversation. "I told him to ask me again in two weeks."

"I will start making plans immediately," Agata said with a smile.

"She did not say she would agree, then."

"But of course she will. You simply have to convince her." Rocco gave his son a significant look. "You've already seduced her into your bed, surely you can induce her to marry you."

Faith felt her cheeks going hot, but Tino did not look in the least bothered. "I intend to try."

"You will succeed," his mother said complacently.

"Will I?" Tino looked at Faith, his gaze trying to decipher something in hers. "That is my hope."

"You know why I want to wait."

"Yes, you do not wish to make the mistake of promising to spend the rest of your life with me in the remote chance it is not a necessary sacrifice."

"It's not me I'm worried about."

"And yet I have made it clear I do not wish to wait to make the commitment."

"You didn't want to marry me before I got pregnant. You didn't even want to be my friend."

"I want to marry you now and I was your friend, if too much of a coward to admit it to my mother." He focused on Agata and Rocco. "I am sorry I was less than truthful with you about my relationship with Faith."

"You lied," Rocco said. No compromise.

Tino nodded, looking pained. *"Si."*

"We forgive you, don't we?" Agata said, giving her husband a transparent look that clearly meant he'd better agree or risk being sent to a guest room for the night.

"Si. You are our son."

And that meant forgiveness. Faith smiled. Maybe Tino had been worried about this. She was glad his parents hadn't drawn it out the way he'd clearly been expecting.

Tino looked no happier, but he said, "Thank you."

"So, do you want a big wedding or something small?" Agata asked.

"I told you—"

Agata cut her son off. "I know what you said, but your father and I have complete faith in you." She looked at Faith expectantly.

"I always dreamed of getting married in a church, with my family there to witness my happiness." She didn't know why she said it. It was a dream that could never be realized.

"I will talk to the father, unless you wish to be married in your Lutheran church?"

Faith shook her head. "I've been attending the Catholic Mass since coming to Sicily. It just felt right."

Agata's face lit up at that. "How wonderful. The father will be very pleased to hear this."

"No doubt," Tino said.

Faith looked at him, a question in her eyes.

He shrugged. "It is one more thing I did not know about you."

"Tino, you know me more deeply than anyone has since Taylish, maybe even better than he did."

Agata glowed at them, while Tino looked almost speechless.

Rocco nodded his head. "As it should be."

While they ate, Agata quizzed Faith on the progress of her pregnancy, wanting to know everything from what doctor she'd gone to see to what her due date was. Tino and Rocco left the conversation to the women for the most part.

They were finished eating when Tino spoke

again. "I will be staying with Faith until she moves home. You will have no problem watching over Giosue for me?"

"Naturally not," Rocco said before Agata could answer.

"But Tino, Gio needs you."

"So do you, even if you will not admit it."

Faith opened her mouth to argue further, but Tino shook his head. "Trust me, I will not neglect my son. I will tuck him in at night and then come to your apartment. If you should be willing to join me in the evenings with Gio, we will both be pleased. I will make sure he knows to invite you."

"You're being sneaky again, Tino." No fair bringing his son into it. "You know I cannot refuse Gio."

"The term is resourceful."

Rocco and Agata laughed.

"I am only relieved my son carried more cache with you than his father."

"That's not true."

"Would you have accepted my invitation so readily?"

She wanted to say yes, if only to prove him wrong, but she couldn't. "We'll discuss this later."

"Already they are talking like an old married couple."

"Don't tease the children, Rocco."

Faith had to laugh at that.

CHAPTER TWELVE

TINO GOT OUT OF THE CAR when they arrived back at Faith's apartment building.

"I don't need an escort to my door, Tino."

"That is no surprise. You do not think you need me for anything."

"I didn't mean that, I just…you don't have to walk me up."

"Perhaps I want to."

She nodded, warmth unfurling through her when he placed his hand on the small of her back even though he was clearly upset with her.

"I do need you, Tino," she said as they climbed the stairs to her second-floor apartment.

"That is good to hear." There was something in his voice that she could not decipher, but he sounded sad…defeated.

Something was definitely wrong.

Hoping to find out what, she offered him a drink when they got upstairs.

But he shook his head. "I must get back to the office if I am going to get out of there at a decent hour tonight."

"Something is bothering you. I want you to tell me what it is."

"It does not matter." He looked away from her. "Life is what it is."

"I don't understand. Are you unhappy I'm pregnant? If you don't want to marry me, I'm not going to make you. And as much as they love you, your parents aren't going to, either."

"I am well aware you are all too ready to walk away from me."

"What? Tino, what has gotten into you? I'm not walking away."

"But you want to."

"No, I don't."

"Oh, you are happy enough to have my baby, but it is clear you would have chosen another father for your child. Only the man you would have chosen is dead."

"I don't want this baby to be Taylish's."

"I do not believe you."

"You are being ridiculous, Tino."

He simply shrugged. "I will see you tonight."

"You do not have to stay with me." She knew he would ignore her, but she had to say it.

"So long as you stubbornly refuse to move home, I do."

"Grisafi Vineyards is not my home."

"It became your home the moment you conceived my child and will remain that way until the day you die, should you wish it. Even if you can never bring yourself to marry me."

"You have no idea how much I want that."

"But not enough to commit to taking me along with it, unless it is proven necessary. Right?"

"Tino, what is going on with you today? That is not what I said and you know it. That is so far from what I feel, it isn't even funny."

"I know that I want you to marry me and that you will not do so."

"You're like a single-track CD programmed to repeat."

He didn't respond.

She had to take a deep breath so she would not yell. He could be so irritating. "Tell me something, Tino."

"*Si?*"

"If I miscarried tomorrow, would you still want to marry me?"

"Yes." His dark eyes gleamed with sincerity and something else. Oh, gosh…it looked like love. He meant it.

Really. Truly.

Her knees went weak, but she could not trust what her brain was telling her heart her eyes were seeing. "You don't mean it."

"I do."

"I…"

"Give us a chance, Faith. You may not love me like you did your precious Taylish, but I can make you happy. You said your attraction to me was a miracle to you."

"It was…it is."

"Marry me, *cuore mio.*"

My heart. He'd called her his heart. Was it a misspoken word, an attempt at manipulation… or did he mean it? "You…I…"

"Please."

She could not deny him. "Promise me something."

"What?"

"You will not regret it."

"This I can easily promise."

"Why?"

"Why would I promise you?"

"Why is it easy?"

"You have not figured it out yet? I have broken my promise to Maura. I love you. You fill my heart. You are my heart."

"You don't. You can't. You said."

"Many things I wished were true, but the only real truth is my love for you."

"But you aren't happy about it."

"I have never before broken a promise. I could not save Maura and now I cannot keep my last promise to her."

"She made you promise never to love again?" That didn't sound like the woman Agata had told Faith about.

"I promised her at her grave. I told her I would never replace her in my heart."

Faith felt the most amazing sense of release pour through her. And she laughed, the joy-filled sound stopping Tino's pacing. "You find the compromise of my honor amusing?"

Instead of answering, she said, "You're being all-or-nothing again. Loving me doesn't mean that Maura no longer has a place in your heart. She has a place in mine, too, because she loved you and because she gave birth to a little boy that I love very much."

"But not his father. I understand. You loved Taylish too much to love another. I should be grateful for what I have. You carry my child and that is a great gift."

"I loved Taylish, but nothing like I love you."

"What do you mean?"

"I loved Taylish, but I was never in love with him. I have been in love with you since the first night we made love."

"You mean that?"

"More than anything."

"I…this is hard."

She grinned. "Talking about your feelings?"

"*Si*. It is not something I like to do."

"You told me you loved me, that's all you needed to say."

"No. You deserve all of the truth."

"What did you leave out?"

"Maura was the love of my youth, you are the love of my life. It hurt when she died. I grieved a long time, but if I lost you, it would kill me."

Faith threw herself at Tino and he caught her, just as she knew he would. They kissed until they were both breathing hard. He pulled his head back, protecting them both from going too far.

She snuggled her head into his neck. "Just one thing, Tino."

"*Si?*"

"Promises made to dead people don't count. They're a way of dealing with our own grief, but when they cause more sadness than consolation, you have to let them go."

"You sound like you know what you are talking about."

"I do. I made a promise to Tay after he died."

"What was it?"

"That I wouldn't try to make a family with

someone else." She sighed and kissed the underside of Tino's jaw. "The promise was for my protection, not his. I made it so I couldn't be hurt again, and when I realized that, I let it go."

"I am glad you were wiser than I."

"I'll remind you that the next time we argue you said that."

"You have my permission, just never remind me what a selfish bastard I was when we were lovers only. I will never forget. But I do not know if I could stand the thought that you won't."

"Tino, we all make mistakes, but real love forgives and forgets."

"You are more than I deserve."

"You just keep believing that, but remember, you are my miracle."

"I love you, *cuore mio*."

"I love you, Tino, more than life."

They married on their one-year anniversary.

Agata had managed to pull together an amazing church wedding and fill said church with family and friends. Faith didn't realize how many friends she'd made in the artistic community and at Gio's school until she saw them all sitting in the pews as she walked up the aisle.

Once her gaze locked on Tino, though, she looked neither to the right nor the left. His expression was filled with love and joy and peace.

It was the peace that made her feel so good. So right.

He was happy to be marrying her, and the guilt he'd felt at loving her was gone now. They'd visited Maura's grave together along with Gio. The trip had seemed to give both males a sense of closure.

Gio was his father's best man, and Agata was Faith's matron of honor. Rocco was giving her away, and the wedding was what she'd always dreamed of and had been sure she could never have. A ceremony celebrating the love and commitment between her and Tino, witnessed by their family.

He had been right about one thing—maybe more than one, but she wasn't telling him that and letting him get a swelled head—that she did have a family now. The Grisafis accepted her as one of their own and unconditionally. Even his brother who lived in New York came home to make her feel welcome and witness his brother's second marriage.

Calogero had insisted on helping Tino by overseeing the transformation of a first-floor room with lots of windows into Faith's new studio. Thereby managing to avoid the brunt of his mother's attempts at changing his single status since returning to Italy. Faith could only be happy that Agata had not made that effort with Tino. Perhaps the older woman had known instinctively her eldest son had already found his second love.

That was all before, though.

Right now Faith hesitated with her hand on the door between the en suite and Tino's— their—bedroom. They had not made love, even when her first trimester had officially ended two weeks before.

Tino had said he wanted to wait for their wedding night. He wanted it to be right. His patience despite his obvious arousal every night when they went to sleep had forever cemented Faith's trust and appreciation for this amazing man she now called husband.

She opened the door and stepped into the bedroom.

Tino stood beside the bed wearing a pair of white silk pajama bottoms.

"White?" she asked with a smile, even though her own lace peignoir was the color of fresh snow.

"It is our first time."

"As husband and wife."

"As a man and a woman who have admitted their love and promised to hold each other in their hearts for a lifetime."

Oh. "I'm going to cry."

"No...you are going to love."

She nodded, too choked up to speak.

He put his arms out. "Come here, *cuore mio*."

She went to him, straight into his arms. He held her there for the longest time, saying nothing. Doing nothing.

Except looking into her eyes, his that dark Hershey-brown that meant his emotions were close to the surface. Finally he said, "Thank you."

"For what?"

"For being mine. For putting up with me. For falling in love with me and not walking away with my baby. For being just who you are, you incredibly precious woman."

The tears rolled then, but they were filled with joy and she made no effort to stop them. "Thank you, Tino, for being mine. For giving me a family again. For being you, but mostly for loving me."

"I will always love you."

"I believe you."

Her fear that she could never have a family was almost completely gone now. His love had given her hope unlike any she'd known since the death of her parents. She'd loved Tay, but she was in love with Tino, and she couldn't help feeling Heaven blessed their union.

His mouth came down on hers, the kiss so incredibly tender and yet sensual, too.

Their tongues played a lazy dance together, getting reacquainted after so much time apart. Their bodies strained together of their own accord as if the very molecules that made up their skin and nerve endings could no longer stand any sort of separation.

Although they had slept curled together for

the past few weeks, she felt the need to relearn his body. She let her hands roam freely over hot, silky flesh covering defined muscles. The hair on his chest rubbed her through her lacey peignoir, reminding her just how susceptible she was to the barest touch by this man.

His rapid heartbeat and heavy breathing said he was equally impacted.

He was no slouch in the caressing department, either, his big hands mapping her body in a way that made her ache deep in her core. She needed him.

He cupped the barely there bump in her stomach. "I have this image of you rounded with my baby, wearing one of my shirts and nothing else while you work on your art."

"Fantasizing, Tino?" she asked with a husky laugh.

"Prophesying, I hope."

"You are silly."

"Because I crave seeing you large with child?"

"It's not exactly sexy."

"So, this is not the time to tell you that the image makes my knees weak with lust."

"Are you serious?"

"I love you, Faith. Seeing you that way, seeing the evidence of our love changing your body— it's the biggest turn-on I've ever known."

"I'll remind you of that when I look like a balloon."

"Trust me, I'm not likely to forget."

"I do trust you, Tino."

"Thank you." Then he kissed her again.

They undressed each other slowly, each treating the other like a treasure to be unwrapped.

Then Tino carried her to the bed and laid her down with tender care. He kissed and caressed her body, gently manipulating her breasts since they were sensitive. She returned the favor, holding the velvet hardness of his arousal with both hands.

"I want you," she whispered.

He nodded, the moment profound as he gave in to her desire.

He made love to her slowly, pleasuring her body and building to the peak of perfect oneness with a measured rhythm that drove her insane and made her feel incredibly cherished all at the same time.

Despite the slow build, her climax surprised her, tightening her body and sending convulsions of pleasure through her. He came a second later, calling out his love.

It was the most perfect moment of Faith's life. She belonged to him completely, just as he belonged to her.

"I love you, Tino. With all my heart and soul."

"*Ti amo,* Faith, who is my heart and reminds me I have a soul."

EPILOGUE

RAFAELLA AGATA GRISAFI was born six months to the day after her parents' marriage. A healthy eight pounds, four ounces, she caused her mother a bit of a problem in the delivery room. Faith was so happy her daughter was healthy and strong, she didn't care how hard the delivery of her precious child had been.

Giosue adored his younger sister and his new mother, often telling anyone who would listen that God must love him an awful lot to give him the best mommy and little sister in the world. Valentino couldn't help agreeing.

He'd lost his first love, but reveled in his second chance at happiness with a woman he looked forward to spending the rest of his life loving.

They were what Faith had always craved—a family.

MILLS & BOON PUBLISH EIGHT LARGE PRINT TITLES A MONTH. THESE ARE THE EIGHT TITLES FOR OCTOBER 2009.

—————————— ○੪ ——————————

THE BILLIONAIRE'S BRIDE OF CONVENIENCE
Miranda Lee

VALENTINO'S LOVE-CHILD
Lucy Monroe

RUTHLESS AWAKENING
Sara Craven

THE ITALIAN COUNT'S DEFIANT BRIDE
Catherine George

OUTBACK HEIRESS, SURPRISE PROPOSAL
Margaret Way

HONEYMOON WITH THE BOSS
Jessica Hart

HIS PRINCESS IN THE MAKING
Melissa James

DREAM DATE WITH THE MILLIONAIRE
Melissa McClone

MILLS & BOON PUBLISH EIGHT LARGE PRINT TITLES A MONTH. THESE ARE THE EIGHT TITLES FOR NOVEMBER 2009.

CR

THE GREEK TYCOON'S BLACKMAILED MISTRESS
Lynne Graham

RUTHLESS BILLIONAIRE, FORBIDDEN BABY
Emma Darcy

CONSTANTINE'S DEFIANT MISTRESS
Sharon Kendrick

THE SHEIKH'S LOVE-CHILD
Kate Hewitt

THE BROODING FRENCHMAN'S PROPOSAL
Rebecca Winters

HIS L.A. CINDERELLA
Trish Wylie

DATING THE REBEL TYCOON
Ally Blake

HER BABY WISH
Patricia Thayer

millsandboon.co.uk Community

Join Us!

The Community is the perfect place to meet and chat to kindred spirits who love books and reading as much as you do, but it's also the place to:

- Get the inside scoop from authors about their latest books
- Learn how to write a romance book with advice from our editors
- Help us to continue publishing the best in women's fiction
- Share your thoughts on the books we publish
- Befriend other users

Forums: Interact with each other as well as authors, editors and a whole host of other users worldwide.

Blogs: Every registered community member has their own blog to tell the world what they're up to and what's on their mind.

Book Challenge: We're aiming to read 5,000 books and have joined forces with The Reading Agency in our inaugural Book Challenge.

Profile Page: Showcase yourself and keep a record of your recent community activity.

Social Networking: We've added buttons at the end of every post to share via digg, Facebook, Google, Yahoo, technorati and de.licio.us.

www.millsandboon.co.uk